A TRUE STORY BASED ON LIES

A TRUE STORY
BASED ON LIES

Jennifer Clement

CANONGATE

First published in Great Britain in 2001 by
Canongate Books Ltd, 14 High Street, Edinburgh EH1 1TE

This edition published in the United States of America
and Canada in 2002

1 3 5 7 9 10 8 6 4 2

British Library Cataloguing in Publication Data

A catalogue record for this book is available upon
request from the British Library

ISBN 1 84195 276 1

Typeset by Palimpsest Book Production Limited,
Polmont, Stirlingshire
Printed and bound in the USA

www.canongate.net

This book is dedicated to Octavia Wiseman

[26]And if a man smite the eye of his servant, or the eye of his maid,
that it perish; he shall let him go free for his eye's sake.
[27]And if he smite out his manservant's tooth, or his maidservant's tooth;
he shall let him go free for his tooth's sake.

The Holy Bible: King James Version
The Second Book of Moses, called Exodus
Chapter 21

EVERY LEAF IS A MOUTH

I am dark, much darker, and so they call me 'Fly'. I don't like to be called 'Fly', but I've accepted it. One has to accept mistakes.

It is only a word.

Fly.

SOME THINGS WERE OVERHEARD AND
SOME SAID IT WAS ALL A RUMOUR

I am a broom-child. My voice sounds like sweeping. Comb, rake, brush, sweep against stone, dirt, and grass. Dry, brittle sound. Scratch. A rasp and scrape without vowels. A long shhhhhhhhh.

Leonora does not have a father. Her mother says, 'All the fingers in our family are buried without wedding rings. Under the ground there are bouquets of fingers without wedding rings.'

Leonora imagines the pale, white bones of her grand-mothers' fingers buried beneath the earth.

A wreath of fingers.

As Leonora walks in her village on the outskirts of Mexico City, she stares at the men to see if any of them look like her. Only the man who sells rabbits and chickens looks like her. Her mother says that her father is in heaven, but that could mean anything since all those things her mother does not want to think about have gone to heaven. Heaven could be a canteen, a field, or the house next door.

Leonora's mother collects twigs for making brooms. These are not the perfect, factory-made brooms that one buys at the supermarket, but the witch-like brooms made from branches that street-sweepers and gardeners use. She and her children spend three weeks out of every month in the mountains looking for the long, brittle sticks. Leonora's mother says that they are all 'broom-children'.

Leonora's brothers and sisters all have Mexican indigenous names. Her sisters are called Mexica and Xochi. Her four brothers are called Moctezuma, Tizoc, Cuautli and Tlaloc. Only Leonora has a Christian, Spanish name. 'Because you wanted to come out so fast,' her mother says. 'You wanted to crack me like an egg.'

Tearing a green stick.

The broom-children are covered with fine pink lines all over their skin.

Their mother whips them with a branch, like mules, to make them walk faster. She ties the twigs to their backs with a plastic clothesline. The twigs cut and scrape their arms and necks.

Leonora's family has been searching for twigs for as long as anyone can remember. Everyone in the family has long, stringy arms as if their bodies had become what they were searching for.

Leonora's mother teaches her children never to speak what they think since this will give them power. She explains that they must keep their voices in their heads like prayers, 'Because one never knows what powerful people are really thinking. One never knows what God is thinking.'

We know how to be quiet. Our thoughts are whispers.
Shhhhhhh.

When Leonora was seven, a man came to their village who said he needed children to help him plant and cut his crop. He promised that he would pay two pesos a day. Most of the village children who were more than six years old went with him. The children waved to their parents and sucked their fingers as they were carried down the dirt road in the back of a dirty, red pick-up truck.

Leonora's mother gave her children a few sticks to be used as a charm and told them to bite the sticks if they wanted to come home. She said, 'Never forget that there are three reasons why the Spaniard conquered Mexico: horses, gunpowder, and smallpox.' She was very proud that all her children had large, coin-shaped scars on their arms from the smallpox vaccinations, as though they had been branded.

For three weeks the children slept in a large barn. There were other children there also and some did not speak Spanish. They gestured with their hands as they spoke in their indigenous dialects.

They say there is no honey in this land.

Every morning and evening the children planted tiny brown seeds in the ground. During the mid-day heat they went back to the barn and slept. Leonora spent long hours biting on the stick that her mother had given to her until it had shred into small pieces and her mouth smelled of pine.

After three weeks, Leonora, and her brothers and sisters, were sent back to their village in the same pick-up truck. Their mother had found out that they were planting marijuana.

After this experience, Leonora's mother decided that she was sick of being tricked. She said, 'I am sick of being tricked.'

Only the cross does not steal because it cannot move its arms.

She decided to send her three daughters to the Saint Cecilia Convent, a ten hour walk from the village. She said she did not want her family to be ignorant, stupid people who gather twigs forever. She kept the boys with her since she had no place to send them.

Leonora and her sisters wrapped their belongings in their sweaters: a hair ribbon, ash leaves, two sticks, an empty plastic coke bottle filled with cinnamon water, and two t-shirts. 'You will learn all about Christ and the Virgin Mary,' their mother said, 'And this will be good. You will learn to wash your clothes and pray before you eat.'

She reminded them to keep quiet and instructed them always to say, 'yes'. 'The word "no" is an obstinate, mule word. A word for small mouths,' she said.

I know the stones bled when the Virgin died.

EVERY LEAF IS A MOUTH

Yesterday my brother, Pedro, kept whispering, 'Buzz, buzz,' every time he came near me. He says 'buzz' because that is the noise a fly makes. He pretends to swat at me with a newspaper and cries, 'Fly!' My mother laughs when I tell her and thinks it's funny, a funny joke. She tells me not to be so sensitive.

Leonora is one of our servants. She has been with us for many years. She came to work in our house even before I was born. My mother hired her from a convent because she needed a nanny for us. Leonora is very long and skinny, like a broomstick, and wears a big, wooden cross around her neck tied to a piece of leather.

The other servants in our house are Sofia and Josefa. Sofia is the cook and also lives here. She shares a room on the roof with Leonora. Josefa is a day-maid who comes every morning to clean the house.

I like Leonora best because she is very kind. When I am unhappy she holds my hand and walks with me out into the garden. We look at the grapefruit tree, which is covered with small fruits. 'Look,' she declares, 'It is a tree of moons.'

Leonora says that I am a 'broom-child', just as she is. She thinks we are dark, like tree bark, and that our arms look like branches and our fingers look like twigs.

I like the way she brushes my hair with seven sticks tied together.

I like it when she sticks spider webs on my cuts and scratches.

I like it when she sings me songs about the three-legged goat.

I like her scent of lemon rind and rice water.

She tells me stones can bleed because there is a heart inside of every stone and rock.

She says the stones bled when the Virgin died.

She says if you listen to a stone you can hear it beat.

SOME THINGS WERE OVERHEARD AND SOME SAID IT WAS ALL A RUMOUR

Leonora lived at the convent until she was thirteen. She learned how to make a bed, wash dishes, iron, knit, and read and write. When she finished her chores, and was not at mass, she spent her time in the convent's orchard. She liked to be outside under the trees.

One day the Mother Superior told Leonora that a family was coming from Mexico City to hire a servant. She explained that she had recommended Leonora to them. Over the years Leonora had watched families arrive at the convent and leave with one of the girls.

'You'll get to eat meat several times a week,' the Mother Superior told Leonora.

Leonora said, 'Yes, Mother.'

Listen for whistles, listen for tambourines. I will walk where I have never walked before and breathe unfamiliar air. I will stand at a window. I will open a door. I will open my hand, open my mouth, and swallow a new house.

'You must always be very polite and never speak what you think,' the Mother Superior continued. 'Today is a lucky day. I'll be sending word to your mother.'

Break a stick. Taste the marrow. Light a candle.

Later that day a new, clean white car driven by a chauffeur arrived at the convent. There was a young woman asleep in the back seat. She had light-brown, curly hair. When the chauffeur parked and opened the door, she woke up, opened her large brown eyes, and stepped out of the car. She had long fingernails coated with red polish and she was wearing a light-blue skirt, a jacket, a white silk blouse, white stockings, and white high-heeled shoes. She wore a two-strand string of pearls that matched her pearl earrings. Her name was Lourdes Camila Fuentes de O'Conner and she was twenty-five years old.

Leonora thought she was very beautiful and clean.

Bark stripped off of wood.

In the car Leonora sat very straight and poised beside Mrs. O'Conner. Leonora had never been in a car before and she liked the fresh smell of the leather seats and Mrs. O'Conner's perfume that smelled like dried apricots.

'I have two sons,' Mrs. O'Conner said. 'They are Pedro,

who is two, and Francisco, who is four. They need someone to play with. You will be their nanny, but I also need you to wash and iron all the clothes.'

'Yes, Mrs. O'Conner,' Leonora said.

She is so clean.

'The house is large and has a garden. You will have a room on the roof that you will share with Sofia. She is the cook. A day-maid comes in everyday to clean. Her name is Josefa.'

'Yes, Mrs. O'Conner,' Leonora said.

She is so soft.

'My husband does not come home for lunch. He is a lawyer and works downtown. Sometimes he does not come home until very late at night. He has meetings. When he does come home for dinner I want the children bathed early and ready for bed so he can be with them before they go to sleep.'

'Yes, Mrs. O'Conner,' Leonora said.

She is like bread.

'You are actually very pretty, but very thin,' Mrs. O'Conner continued. 'My, you have very long arms! I told the nuns I wanted someone pretty for my boys. What size are you? I'll get you your uniform this week. Blue should look good on you – light blue with your dark skin. Your hands have to be clean at all times. You must wash your hands after you go to the toilet. I have been told by the nuns that you know this. Still, I have to tell you this: you must wash your hands after you go to the toilet and after you eat and I still expect you to wash them at least another five times during the day.'

'Yes, Mrs. O'Conner,' Leonora said.

Clean, soft bread.

'Every three months we will take you to Dr. Morales. He has a laboratory. He will check to make sure that you do not have parasites. On the first visit he'll check you for tuberculosis and he'll check your throat too. I have to protect my boys.'

'Yes, Mrs. O'Conner,' Leonora said.

The land will not be fallow. The rain will come.

'You have Sundays off. However, we expect you to be back at the house by six in time to help with the supper. Sometimes I might ask you to help serve the table if we have invited guests over. The nuns have told me that you know how. You serve from the left and take away from the right, correct?'

Mrs. O'Conner closed her eyes and leaned her head against the window and soon was asleep. Leonora looked at Mrs. O'Conner's hands. She wore a large diamond ring and a wedding band.

Bouquets of fingers.

Leonora had never been to Mexico City before. She looked out the window while Mrs. O'Conner slept beside her. There were large billboards with the faces of television actors on them. Leonora thought that on those faces one tooth alone must be the size of a house.

Brick walls, stone walls, cement walls, adobe walls.
There is no honey in this land.

The grey colour of concrete was reflected in the sky.

The O'Conner house was very large and painted salmon pink. Leonora's room on the roof looked down on the garden where there was a large grapefruit tree and a pond filled with yellow fish. The room had two single beds and was filled with objects belonging to Sofia, the cook. Sofia had made an altar to the Virgin of Guadalupe in one corner of the room with plastic flowers and candles surrounding it. She had also stuck newspaper clippings from the social pages on the wall. They were photographs of the O'Conners at benefits, weddings and cocktail parties.

On the roof there was also a washroom and a laundry-room. Mrs. O'Conner gave Leonora a plastic bag filled with rubber gloves, powdered soap, and two long, blue plastic ropes to use as clotheslines.

The house tastes like tangerines, yellow plastic buckets, and linseed oil. It smells of soap and coriander.

Mrs. O'Conner introduced Leonora to Sofia, a stout, middle-aged woman whose front teeth had been capped with gold. She also introduced Leonora to the day-maid, Josefa, who was a short woman with black, straight hair and oriental features. Josefa was cross-eyed.

Then Mrs. O'Conner took Leonora to meet the boys. They were playing in a large room filled with toys, a television, and a small swing set. The room opened on to the garden. Francisco and Pedro looked like their mother although their skin was much lighter and covered with freckles.

That night, lying in bed, Sofia asked Leonora where she had come from. 'I used to gather twigs. I was a broom-girl and then I was lucky and went to the convent. Now I am here.' Leonora answered.

Bite a twig if you want to come home.

'This is a good family,' Sofia said. 'You're lucky. If you work well you could not find a better place. You are lucky as there will be no more children. Mrs. O'Conner cannot have any more since something went wrong when Francisco was born. It will be easy for you with just two. I think I've been treated well. I've never known anything else.'

Over the next few days Mrs. O'Conner and Sofia taught Leonora what she had to do. She did not speak to Josefa, the day-maid, very much since Josefa answered everything with one word. If Leonora asked her where the towels were kept Josefa said, 'Fair'. If Leonora asked her where she lived, Josefa said, 'Correction'. If Leonora asked her when the chauffeur was coming home with the diapers, Josefa would say, 'Clock'.

What Leonora liked best was the night time.

Talking about the day time.

She liked listening to Sofia talk before they fell asleep.

Starched, white aprons hang over chairs.

Sofia smelled like garlic, cumin and oregano. She picked

at her gold teeth with a toothpick. Before going to sleep Sofia rubbed her face with a lemon to bleach her skin and then the room smelled of lemons for the rest of the night. Sofia could talk non-stop without taking a breath.

A shadow does not move.

On the second night after Leonora's arrival at the house, Sofia said, 'You are still white, like a page nobody has written on, but I am a book. Everything has happened to me. I have even tasted a lot of things like stuffed olives, squid, and caviar. Caviar is the most expensive food in the world, more expensive than gold. I didn't like it. It was like eating pebbles of salt. I really don't like to eat any kind of egg. Once, years ago, I was making breakfast for Mrs. O'Conner's mother (that is where I used to work so I've known Mrs. O'Conner since she was little) and there was a chick inside the egg with feathers and everything. I knew that was a bad omen and, as it turned out, it was. The next day they killed the students. They cut them down like trees. This was in 1968. My friend Concha's boyfriend went there and stole all the dead students' shoes. He took them off those dead students and sold them. He gave me a pair, but I have never worn them. I had to clean the blood off of them. Can you imagine he sold them with the blood? How could you steal the shoes of dead people? When I said this to him he said that shoes did not have feelings. Well, they give me feelings, I said to him.

I know about feelings. Mrs. O'Conner's brother was killed in an aeroplane crash. I went with her mother to the airport and that was the last time she ever spoke. Her last words were spoken to me. We were in an office with other families who were waiting for the news and she said, "Hold my hand". Then a man came in and told us it was true and she never spoke again. Her mouth became a big O, like a cave. You can see this in the photographs Mrs. O'Conner has in her bedroom if you don't believe me. There is a picture of her holding Francisco as a baby and you can see her mouth, a big O.

The priest told her to forget her son and have another. He said God made women to have lots of babies so that if they lose one or two it does not matter. I also saw some soldiers saying that on the television news after they had killed some babies, but that was in Africa.'

The house bends over me and carries my feet when I walk. The stairs lift me up and hold me high.

EVERY LEAF IS A MOUTH

Leonora tells my brothers that if they stop calling me 'Fly' and call me by my real name, which is Aura, she's going to buy them a present.

Leonora has learned everything she knows from Sofia. She rubs lemons on my skin and says that my name sounds like a deep well: Aura. She says someone might try to climb inside me, so she rubs my lips with cloves. Every time I go up to her room on the roof she tells me to get out because my mother does not like me to spend so much time in the servants' room.

From Leonora's room I can see our garden. I imagine that I am in an aeroplane looking down on everything. I can see our pond, with the goldfish shinning like bright specs in the water, and the grapefruit tree.

Leonora says that there are hot and cold people. She says that hot people drive bees away because they don't like heat and that a cold person cannot light a fire. We are both hot people.

Ice always melts in my hands.

Leonora likes to brush my hair with twigs. She sings to me and ties my hands behind my back to keep them still.

I have hands that do different things. My doctor calls this the 'Strange Hand Syndrome' or the 'Autonomous Hand Syndrome'. It comes from the French '*Main etranger*'. It means that sometimes the two halves of my brain are working independently. My mother says she noticed this when one of my hands opened a drawer and the other hand closed it. When I was little she used to tell me to keep my left hand in my pocket. It never wanted to stay there.

Sofia says that they always looked different. When I was born she remembers that the right hand looked like a pine cone and the left looked like a leaf.

Josefa says, 'Clam.'

Leonora adds that it does not matter because I have two rivers running inside of me and that will both end at the sea.

The doctors said that playing a musical instrument might help me so my mother bought me a piano. She has hired a piano teacher to come to the house twice a week. I think it is very easy. Leonora likes the piano very much and dusts it twice a day.

My right hand plays the black keys and my left hand plays the white ones.

Josefa says, 'Teeth.'

SOME THINGS WERE OVERHEARD AND
SOME SAID IT WAS ALL A RUMOUR

Innocent little dove, you have let yourself be fooled, knowing that on this day you should lend nothing.

Six days later Leonora met Mr. O'Conner for the first time. She had been playing ball in the garden with the boys and they were now lying together beside the pond looking at the fish. Francisco had taken the ribbon out of Leonora's hair and was trying to tie it into his own while Pedro threw handfuls of grass into the water.

Leonora did not know how long Mr. O'Conner had been watching them when Francisco jumped up and ran over to greet his father.

Mr. O'Conner was sitting on the lawn under the large grapefruit tree that grew beside the door leading into the garden. He was formally dressed in a navy blue suit and a red, paisley silk tie. Leonora recognised him immediately from Sofia's newspaper clippings and the photographs that were scattered around the house on the mahogany tables and the walls in the main hall.

Mr. O'Conner had red hair, blue eyes and very white, freckled skin. He was the grandson of an Irishman who had come to Mexico in the late 1800s. This grandfather had discovered a silver mine, which had made the family very wealthy. However, like many other immigrants living in Mexico, there was nothing Irish about him. Even his English had a Spanish accent.

While he spoke to his children, hugging and kissing them, Leonora noticed that he had a long, pink scar that began under his ear and moved down the side of his left cheek. He looked about ten years older than Mrs. O'Conner.

After greeting the children, he looked up at Leonora and beckoned to her with his hand. Leonora walked over to him.

'Do you like my boys?' he asked. 'They are good boys, don't you think?'

'Yes, sir,' Leonora answered.

'You have to make sure that Pedro eats enough, and make sure he drinks his milk, which he does not like. He always looks thin to me,' he continued.

'Yes, sir,' Leonora said.

Mr. O'Conner stood up and brushed his trousers with

his hands. Then he looked around the garden. 'I have not been out here for a while,' he said. 'That tree needs to be pruned. It's tall enough now for a swing.'

He did not wait for an answer and, holding the children by the hand, turned around and went with them into the house.

Leonora stood alone under the grapefruit tree for a few minutes and then went back inside the house.

Until tomorrow.

That night in bed, lying in the dark, Leonora told Sofia she had finally met Mr. O'Conner that afternoon.

'Mr. O'Conner adores his children,' Sofia said. 'He also loves his wife but everyone knows he has a mistress. He leaves early and comes back late. The chauffeur once told me that it was a woman from Guadalajara. The women from there are very beautiful and have French blood.'

'Oh,' Leonora said.

'Mrs. O'Conner knows, of course,' Sofia continued, 'but she is a smart lady and keeps her mouth shut. You can tell it hurts her, but she has her boys and look at this house! Anyway, if she makes a fuss he'll only deny it and get angry, so what is the point? She knows this.

This woman is not the first. He has had many. I know he even had someone when they were engaged. But this is not so bad. Men have their needs. We all know that.'

'How did he get that scar?' Leonora asked. 'It is very ugly.'

'Oh, that is nothing,' Sofia answered. 'He was duelling with his brother when he was a child and his brother's sword cut his cheek.'

I want to go to your country so you may sing your songs to me.

'They had swords?' Leonora asked.

'Oh, dear, no,' Sofia exclaimed. 'It was long ago. They were playing with some branches in the garden.'

Everyone finds a tree.

'He really spoils those two boys,' Sofia continued. 'But then Mrs. O'Conner does the same. Where I come from, children are kept wrapped up until they are two years old. There are no children walking around and thinking that the world belongs to them. We also know that whipping children makes them strong. My mother used to hit me with a shoe. It is different in the city, but rich people are different anyway.'

'I used to be hit with a stick or a shredded twig. Then I used to go outside and eat little stones I found in the gravel on the road. I looked for pebbles that had colours in them. My mother used to say that one day my stomach was going to hurt. Then the doctors would have to open my stomach and take out all the stones,' Leonora said.

The dry taste of a stone covered in dust. The cool taste of a blue pebble. Rock like ice. Rock like salt. The taste of sun and clay. A riverbed inside.

EVERY LEAF IS A MOUTH

When I was still very small, Francisco killed the two baby ducks that Leonora had given us. She'd bought them from a man who came to the front door selling ducks and rabbits. We called them 'Ping' and 'Pong'. We kept them in the garden in a large green plastic tub under the grapefruit tree. Leonora said that when they grew older they could swim in the pond.

One day, after school, Francisco went out to the garden alone and plucked all their feathers off. After doing this, he hung them from a tree. He used a piece of the clothesline and hung them by their necks. Then, he hit them with a broom stick as if they were Christmas piñatas filled with tangerines and peanuts.

Later that afternoon Sofia found the ducks and began to scream. They were split to shreds and there was blood all over the grass. Leonora heard Sofia's cries and ran out to the garden. She cut down the ducks and buried them in the garden before my mother came home.

My mother said that this is what children do, but I would never have done that. I cannot imagine killing anything.

Leonora told me that anything you kill goes right into you and stays there forever.

I know that Francisco still has those ducks inside of him.

Two years ago, a policeman killed our gardener who came here twice a week to do our garden work. I know that policeman is full of grass and earth and snails.

SOME THINGS WERE OVERHEARD AND SOME SAID IT WAS ALL A RUMOUR

After two years of working and sharing a room together Leonora and Sofia were close friends. Leonora was now fifteen and had changed from a young adolescent into a woman. She wore her hair in two long black braids down her back and rubbed her skin with lemons just like Sofia did. Sofia also taught her to steal the linen napkins from the dining room, or Mr. O'Conner's socks, to use when she was menstruating.

Boat of silver, how silently you glide away from the old shore. White sea gulls, white handkerchiefs.

The first Christmas, after her arrival at the O'Conner's house, Leonora returned to her village to see her family. She had not been home since she had been sent away to the convent. She had only spoken to her mother on a few occasions when her mother would walk an hour to get to a public telephone at another village.

At home Leonora found that all of her brothers had left the village and illegally crossed the border into the United States to find work. In fact, there were very few young men left in the village. Her mother said that her brothers were in Michigan working in a slaughterhouse that provided meat for restaurants. Her two sisters had left the convent and were back in the village. They continued to help their mother gather the twigs for brooms; but spoke about leaving to go and work in factories at the border.

Their mother had bought a small black and white television with the wages Leonora sent home every month. When her mother and sisters were not gathering twigs, they spent most of the day watching soap operas. They told Leonora that their favourite soap opera was 'Lucky Lucia', which was about a young woman who left the countryside and went to Mexico City to be a servant. In a market 'Lucky Lucia' was discovered by a movie director and became a famous actress.

'We always think of you when we watch it,' one of Leonora's sisters said.

Both of Leonora's sisters were pregnant and the fathers of their babies had also gone to the United States.

Tell the little cow she has a calf at her feet and she is breeding another. Tell the little cow to come down to the road. She has a calf at her feet and she is breeding another.

A few days later, Leonora's mother told her that, one

year ago, she had had a child. 'Of course, I buried the umbilical cord under an ash tree,' her mother said. 'But nothing helped. The baby was born crooked and gnarled and died three days later.'

'It is because she drinks so much mescal,' one of Leonora's sisters explained. 'And then she does not know who she is.'

'It is because she lies down with anyone,' Leonora's other sister added, 'like a street dog.'

During the two weeks that Leonora stayed in her village a few men used to come to the house at night and stand outside the door. They brought gifts of rice or beans and bottles of rum or mescal. They'd take off their straw hats and knock on the door whispering, 'Let me in, let me in.'

Leonora's mother would walk to the door and call out, 'Go away old goats, can't you see, I am with my daughters!'

Whisper. Wind. Angel bless this house.
Let me in.

The following Christmas Leonora decided to stay in

Mexico City with Sofia while the O'Conner family went on their annual skiing holiday.

'You really should go home,' Sofia said as the three servants were sitting in the kitchen eating cheese mixed with coriander, tomatoes and onions. 'Your sister's children must be three hands high by now.'

'No,' Leonora answered. 'I'd rather stay here.'

Taste the marrow.

'Daybreak,' Josefa said, who never spoke more than one word at a time.

'Josefa and I are going to go and have a cleansing. You can come too if you like,' Sofia said. 'We do this every Christmas so that we may be clean and pure for the new year.'

'Rabbit,' Josefa agreed.

The next day, Leonora, Josefa and Sofia took a bus to a large market in the centre of the city. Sofia led them through the stands of oranges, pomegranates, and bananas, and past the stalls that were festooned with Christmas lights, and piñatas in the shape of blue, green and gold stars. There were stands that sold small clay figures of Christ in a manger surrounded by clay animals, clay angels, and clay figures of the Three Kings. The market was filled with the scent of the pine trees and peanuts.

At the back of the market there was a stall covered and enclosed with a thick, chequered blanket.

'Here we are,' Sofia said, and called out, 'Mister Novino, Mister Novino are you there?'

A man peeked out through the side of the blanket. He had a thick, black moustache, and wore a white laboratory coat over his clothes.

He held out his palm and each of the women paid him ten pesos.

Sofia went in first, while Leonora and Josefa waited outside. The man's cubicle was right beside the meat stalls and the smell of the raw meat hanging from thick, metal hooks permeated the atmosphere. Josefa covered her nose with her sleeve.

When Sofia had finished she came out of the man's stand looking radiant. Then it was Josefa's turn.

'He is a master,' Sofia said. 'There is no one better. People come from all over Mexico to see him. He said I was very clean and pure and that I had not swallowed anything bad all year. The word he used was "transparent" like "glass".'

When Josefa came out of the stall she bowed her head and said, 'Fur'. Then she held the blanket open so that Leonora could go in.

Inside the stall there were three candles lit before a statue of the Virgin Mary. The man told Leonora to take off her sweater and sit on a stool. He sprinkled some water on her and began to hit her arms and legs with some long-stemmed carnations. When he had finished hitting her, he picked up a lemon and carved the shape of a cross into it with one of his fingernails. Then, he picked up an egg and rubbed it all over her body. He placed his hand, with the egg in it, into Leonora's blouse and rubbed her breasts, stomach and back. After he had finished, he broke the egg and dropped the white and yolk into a glass of water. He said that the egg had consumed her spirit and that he was going to 'read' what it said.

After examining the glass of water filled with yolk and egg white he sighed and said that the egg looked like a snake, which was a sure indication that she had been taken over by air spirits.

Brooms on stone. Brooms on grass and brick.

He told Leonora to beat her back with branches to make

the spirits go away and to pray for all the virgin animals. He also told her never to say aloud what she was thinking or things she ate would turn cold in her mouth. He also said that for this next year she must pray for cobblers and iron-welders.

Timorous body why get frightened? Cowardly body, don't be afraid. May she not die in childbirth, may she not die of fright, may she not die without confession; may that fright fall in the ocean, may it fall into the mountains, may it seize another unfortunate.

Afterward Sofia reported that the man had not 'read' her egg but was going to bury it. 'He said this will keep me transparent.'

When Leonora said that the man told her she was filled with air spirits Josefa said, 'Celery.'

The virgin deer. The virgin cow. The virgin dog.

Sofia told Leonora to do what the man had said. 'This is a very grave symptom. It is worse than a disease,' Sofia said. 'It is a good thing that you did not go home. You needed to know this. I knew one woman who had this and her left arm turned into a hard stick and never moved again. It was so dry she had to rub oil on it four or five times a day. She always wore long sleeves, but you could tell since it was so stiff.'

Josefa said, 'Glass.'

'Yes,' Sofia answered. ' You must breathe on glass.'

Breathe on glass. Breathe into the cup of your hand. Pray for cobblers and iron-welders. Pray for all virgin animals.

EVERY LEAF IS A MOUTH

Everyone in the house has to be very quiet. My mother sleeps all the time. We walk on tip-toe and whisper. She sleeps all day and wakes up at night. Leonora says that my mother's life is moving backward, and that her life is inside out.

My mother says she likes to be awake when everyone is asleep and that she likes to be asleep when everyone is awake. Leonora says it is because she wishes every day of the week were Sunday.

Once I woke her up. I was running and I slipped on the stairs. I hit my elbow against the banister and there was blood all over my arm and I needed four stitches.

Leonora found me first. She held me in her arms and licked the tears off my cheeks as she rocked me back and forth. She has always licked my tears. She drinks them to keep me inside of her. Mothers always do this in her village.

My cries woke up my mother and she came out of her

bedroom to see what had happened. My mother slapped Leonora weakly across her face. In a very soft, but angry voice, she said, 'Get away from my daughter. I've told you to keep away from her. Do you want to pack your bags this minute?'

'No, no!' Leonora answered and ran out of the room.

After I came back from the doctor's office my mother went back to sleep, and I went up to the roof to the servants' room.

Leonora was sitting on her bed hitting her arms with some sticks. Sofia was crouched beside her saying, 'That is enough now, that is enough.'

Leonora put the sticks under her pillow.

'You must stop eating salt and pepper,' Sofia said. 'You need to sweeten your blood. Then insects will bite you again.'

When Leonora and Sofia saw me standing at the door they both stood up. Sofia took my hand and lay me down on her bed. 'Did the stitches hurt?' she asked.

Leonora sat beside me and kissed my forehead.

One of my hands rubbed my hair and the other slapped

my leg. Leonora left the room and came back in with a clothesline. She tied my arms to the bed and said, 'I understand. A part of you wants to walk and a part of you wants to run.'

'Why does my mother hate Leonora so much?' I asked Sofia.

'Because Leonora is filled with air spirits,' Sofia answered.

'Not any more. Not any more. I've made them go away. I've swept them out of me.' Leonora answered.

'What are air spirits?' I asked.

'It just means that you are hollow and that air can blow into you.' Sofia answered. 'But I am sure that they are practically all gone by now. She has been doing everything she was told to do.'

After this, I stayed away from Leonora for a while. I was afraid that I might breathe in and swallow her air spirits. I sat far away from her at the kitchen table, and no longer let her sit with me when I had a bath. When she tried to rub my arm or touch my hair I ran away, even if this made her sad.

Sofia said that I was acting ridiculous because the air spirits are not contagious.

Today the piano teacher came to give me a lesson. I learned how to play a new scale. Leonora said that it sounded very nice and reminded her of church music.

Josefa said, 'Teeth.'

Sofia said that she likes it best when I play the black keys because they sound like old sounds.

Leonora agreed.

Josefa said, 'Ladder.'

SOME THINGS WERE OVERHEARD AND SOME SAID IT WAS ALL A RUMOUR

Now that the boys were older and going to school, Mrs. O'Conner began working mornings at a nearby orphanage. Sofia, Josefa, and Leonora enjoyed having the house to themselves. They turned the radio on and drank coffee together. Sometimes Leonora would bring the ironing board downstairs and work in the kitchen while Sofia cooked.

Leonora was very careful as she ironed Mr. O'Conner's shirts that were all made of silk or 100 per cent cotton.

Sometimes she used a little spit.

Spit and water.

Sofia liked to spend this time talking about her childhood.

'When I was little,' Sofia said, 'there were no buses; we had trams. You could meet people on trams, but you cannot meet people on buses. My mother met my father on a tram. He liked to buy her coconuts. He said this would give her many children, but she only had me. He worked for the oil company, Pemex, at one of its refineries. Once there was a fire and he was badly burned. You could not even see his face any more. My mother said he looked like a worm. He lived for six days.'

'Larva,' Josefa said.

'Yes,' Sofia answered. 'My mother said he looked like a worm or white larva.'

'Termite,' Josefa said.

'My mother was a seamstress. She made clothes for actors in the movies. She died when I was six. She liked to wear very small shoes to make her feet look small. She was a size four, but she would wear a size two. She died from gangrene that grew in one of her toes. Then I lived with my aunt, Chula, who was also a seamstress, and when I was ten I began working for this family.'

'Yams,' Josefa said.

'I met Rodrigo when I was fifteen. He was the young man who came around on Saturdays selling yams from a cart. He made me feel alive. He would kiss me for ten minutes without stopping. I felt my whole body in my mouth. I used to see him on Sundays, my day off. He said he wanted to marry me, but a year later I found out that he was already married. I couldn't eat for four months and never ate yams again.'

I feel my whole body in my mouth. My legs, arms and hands are in my mouth. My liver and spleen are in my mouth. My breasts are in my mouth.

'My aunt Chula is very lucky. She worked in the building that fell down during the earthquake. Do you remember that factory where all the seamstresses worked?' Sofia continued. 'Well, she did not go to work that day since she woke up feeling dizzy. All her friends died.'

'Kites,' Josefa said.

'Yes,' Sofia said. 'A few days later we went to that building. It was a tomb. We took flowers. There were dozens and dozens of dresses and blouses hanging from the trees and electrical wires. They looked like kites.'

Empty clothes. Scarecrow. Arms and legs made of branches. A broomstick is a spine. A leaf is a mouth.

On Sundays, her day off, Leonora would go to mass with Sofia in the morning. Then they would spend the rest of the day in the Alameda Park shopping for hair clips, samplers, and comic books written for adults. At six o'clock they went back to the house in time for supper.

One night as Leonora and Sofia were lying in bed Sofia said, 'I am becoming like a young woman again. I've been bleeding all day.'

By four in the morning, Sofia was moaning and sighing. Leonora turned on the light. She looked at Sofia who's brown skin had turned red with fever. Leonora rose out of bed and realised that she was standing in a small pool of Sofia's blood.

'I'm going to go and get Mrs. O'Conner,' Leonora said and went downstairs and knocked on the O'Conner's bedroom door.

Mrs. O'Conner went up to the servants' room on the roof and wrapped Sofia in a blanket. Then Mr. O'Conner came up also. He carried Sofia downstairs in his arms, and placed her in his car. Mrs. O'Conner decided to stay with the children and told Leonora to go with Mr. O'Conner and Sofia to the nearby government clinic.

In the car Sofia continued to sigh and moan. Leonora sat beside her in the back seat and quietly rubbed her arm.

Don't be afraid. You are the sailor's guide. Today I come to greet you, greeting your beauty in your celestial reign.

At the clinic Sofia was placed on a stretcher and taken into the emergency room. Leonora and Mr. O'Conner were told to go and sit in the waiting room and wait for the doctor.

Leonora was still wearing the white, flannel slip she used as a nightgown and blue plastic sandals. Mr. O'Conner was dressed in trousers and a sweater.

As time passed, Leonora began to tremble and shake with fear and cold. Mr. O'Conner took off his sweater and told her to put it on. Leonora put it on, but shook even more. Leonora thought his sweater smelled like camomile tea.

'Your arms are so long,' Mr. O'Conner said. 'I'd never noticed that before.'

Leonora folded her arms across her chest.

'How long has Sofia been bleeding like this?' he continued.

'I can't say,' Leonora answered.

The broom-children are out there asleep under a tree. They are surrounded by bundles of twigs tied with yarn. This night also belongs to them.

Mr. O'Conner and Leonora sat quietly for over an hour until a doctor finally came in and told them that Sofia was hemorrhaging and that they had given her a blood transfusion. He said that they would have to keep her there for a few days since they needed to run some tests.

Leonora and Mr. O'Conner drove back to the house through the city without saying a word.

In this city there is no darkness, or night. Nowhere to see the moon and stars. There are no night sounds. There is no place to hide.

As they approached the house, Leonora took off Mr. O'Conner's sweater and placed it on the seat between them.

Hide beneath an arm.

'Thank you,' she said. He nodded his head without looking at her.

I can cup my hands over my eyes.

Back in her room, Leonora cleaned up the blood and placed Sofia's sheets in cold water. Then she took some branches out from under her bed and hit her arms with them. She was thinking, 'Please, dear God, don't let Sofia die. Please.'

The night is in my hands.

She scratched the scar of her smallpox vaccination until it bled.

Sweet Virgin, please.

Leonora lit the four candles surrounding Sofia's altar to the Virgin of Guadalupe.

What can I bring to this place?

EVERY LEAF IS A MOUTH

Leonora told me that long ago Sofia had become very sick and almost died. This was before I was born. Leonora says that my father had taken Sofia to a clinic where she stayed for many days and that this was the first time that Leonora had ever slept alone. She said that it felt like it must feel to die and that all the sounds around her became very large: a cricket sounded like a dog, a dog sounded like a truck, a truck sounded like an aeroplane, and an aeroplane sounded like thunder.

I said that this was impossible. Leonora said that everything is possible when you sleep alone.

Because I'm the only girl, I have always slept alone. Once the shadow from my lamp looked like a squirrel. Leonora says that when you sleep alone and you are rich it is very different, more like a game than terror.

When I try to fall asleep, one of my hands lies calmly beneath my head and the other reaches for the lamp and turns it on and off, opens the window, and reaches for a book. Some nights Leonora ties this hand to my side with a piece of a clothesline. This helps.

I've been taken to see all kinds of doctors. They even took me to a specialist in Houston, Texas. She said my condition was very rare, and that it was still being studied. She made me open and close 115 drawers and filmed me at night when I was sleeping. They say that when I'm asleep, one hand rises up into the air and shakes.

This is another reason why my brothers call me 'Fly', because one hand is always flying all over the place. My brothers swat at my hand. My mother says, 'Stop it!' My father catches it and kisses it. Leonora ties it up or rubs it with sticks. Sofia says someday she is going to take me to see a healer, called Moses. She says he is also an animal psychic and can help find animals that you have lost.

Josefa just looks at me and says, 'Daughter.'

No one can figure out where Josefa lives and where she comes from. Because she is cross-eyed, I think she must see two of everything. Maybe she sees two moons in the sky. This is very possible since every time she picks something up she leans over and picks it up again, even though the thing is not there any more. I've watched her make the same bed twice. She puts two spoons of sugar in her coffee. She braids her hair four times. She crosses herself twice.

Sofia says there is no question about it, 'Josefa lives in a world of twos and fours.'

One day I asked Josefa if she saw two of everything. She pointed to her eyes and said, 'Reptile.'

Then I asked her where she was from and she said, 'Breakfast.'

Sometimes Sofia understands her, but I never do. Leonora says that Josefa only speaks with one word because she is full of ideas and thoughts, and is actually very smart.

Sofia treats Josefa very well. She makes sure Josefa is never hungry or thirsty. Sofia gives her food wrapped in napkins to take home. Josefa arrives for work in the morning with an empty plastic bag and leaves with it full. Once I even saw toilet paper in there, along with chicken bones.

'Everyone expects you to steal a bit,' Sofia says, 'otherwise you are not respected.'

SOME THINGS WERE OVERHEARD AND SOME SAID IT WAS ALL A RUMOUR

Sofia stayed at the clinic for two weeks. When Josefa heard what had happened to Sofia she said, 'Premonition', and did not come back to the house for a little over two weeks.

'This is typical of Josefa,' Mrs. O'Conner said. 'When I need her most she disappears. She always comes back, though. And when I ask her what happened she just says, "Well."'

While Sofia and Josefa were gone, Mrs. O'Conner told Leonora that she would have to take charge of everything.

'You'll have to make the beds and cook a bit,' Mrs. O'Conner said. 'And don't forget to take out the rubbish every morning so it does not smell up the house.'

'Yes,' Leonora said.

'I'll be gone all morning but I'll be back by lunch time

with the boys to give you a hand,' Mrs. O'Conner continued. 'Remember do not let anyone into the house. Always ask who it is before you open the door.'

'Yes,' Leonora answered.

The house was very quiet and, for the first time, Leonora knew what it was like to be alone. She had never been alone in her village or at the convent and she was always with someone at the O'Conner's house. Leonora heard her own thoughts, which sounded like voices around her. The songs that she had learned as a child, and had not thought of for years, came back to her, chiming through her mind.

Crystal dove, glass dove, dove made from a window pane. I do not want to break you. I do not want to break you. Crystal dove I do not want you in pieces, broken on the floor.

One morning after Sofia and Josefa had been gone for three days, Mr. O'Conner returned to the house. Only Leonora was home since it was early in the morning and the children were at school and Mrs. O'Conner was still at the orphanage.

Leonora was on the roof hanging sheets on the clothesline, and listening to the songs in her mind.

If the dog barks: listen.
If the cat cries: listen.
If the birds sing: listen.

Leonora heard footsteps coming up to the roof. She turned and saw Mr. O'Conner. She dried her wet hands on her apron and waited for him to speak.

Mr. O'Conner leaned against the large, cement cistern for a few minutes, and then turned around and left.

The doors creak.
The windows murmur.
The floors whisper.
Everything speaks.

The next day the same thing happened while Leonora was in the kitchen cutting green tomatoes and chopping fresh coriander. This time Mr. O'Conner stood in the doorway staring at her. Leonora could hear him breathe. She could hear the knife slicing the tomatoes. She could hear her own heart.

She could hear, softly in her mind, the psalms she had learned at the convent.

Like a tree planted by the rivers of water.

The next day, as Leonora made the beds and swept

the patio, she moved around the house expecting Mr. O'Conner to appear again, but he did not.

I hear a sweet voice. I hear a voice in the trees. It is not the breeze. It is not the sound of wings.
The statues of the Lord are right, rejoicing the heart.

On the sixth day after Sofia and Josefa had left, Leonora was washing the breakfast dishes in the kitchen when Mr. O'Conner came up and stood behind her. She felt him step on her shadow as if he had stepped on the train of a dress.

He stepped on her shadow and stopped her from moving. He put his mouth against her hair and she could hear and feel his warm breath. He circled his arms around her and held her breasts. Then he let go of her and left.

Let the words of my mouth.

On the seventh and eighth day Mr. O'Conner stepped on Leonora's shadow. He lifted her up and carried her on his hip to the bedroom. He placed a towel on the bed first.

There is no speech nor language where their voice is not heard.

On the ninth day he licked her neck.

Blessed be my rock.

On the tenth day he sucked her hair.

To bleed the blackness out and clean its dark, dark smell of bark and monkey.

On the eleventh day again, on the twelfth day again, and on the thirteenth day again.

I may tell all my bones: they look and stare upon me.

All this happened in silence.

> *Quiet, peace. Close your eyes*
> *and don't open them*
> *until I tell you.*

On the evening of the thirteenth day Sofia came back from the clinic.

On the fourteenth day Josefa returned also.

When Mrs. O'Conner asked Josefa why she had left once again without saying anything, and especially when she needed her most, Josefa sucked on her fingers and said, 'Baptism.'

Mrs. O'Conner said she was pleased to have Josefa and

Sofia back since Leonora had broken four glasses and two plates in the last few days.

'You break everything,' Mrs. O'Conner said. 'And you put too much salt in the food. I sometimes think that you are trying to poison us with all that salt!'

Be not far from me; for trouble is near; for there is none to help.

EVERY LEAF IS A MOUTH

Leonora taught me the song about the man who silenced the knife, the knife the bull, the bull the water, the water the fire, the fire the stick, the stick the dog, the dog the cat, the cat the mouse, the mouse the spider, the spider the fly, the fly the frog that was singing under the water.

I like to tell her all about science and mathematics since Leonora likes to know about everything that I learn at school. I teach her that Pancho Villa had a horse called Lucifer, and she laughs. I tell her that clouds are evaporated rivers, and she laughs. I explain to her that fossils are the stone moulds of things that were once alive, and she laughs. I tell her that subtract means to 'take away'. When she says goodnight to me she says she will, 'subtract herself from me.'

Leonora says that there are many things she knows that I don't. She says that there is a wooden cross inside of every tree. She says that clouds are water ghosts. She says that fossils come from the moon.

I tell Leonora there are three categories for things: alive, dead, and never alive. She answers that I am mistaken.

She says that there are more categories than that. 'What about never dead? What about living dead? What about half-alive?' she asks.

When Leonora kisses me goodnight, she draws a cross on my forehead with her finger and says, 'I am the memory of your future.'

SOME THINGS WERE OVERHEARD AND
SOME SAID IT WAS ALL A RUMOUR

28 days.

After the operation Sofia said, 'This has always been true, but now it is worse: I hear the pale voices of my unborn children.'

28 stairs to the roof.

Leonora never told Sofia what had happened between her and Mr. O'Conner and, as soon as everyone was back in the house, her secret encounters with Mr. O'Conner ceased.

Mr. O'Conner often stared at Leonora. She could feel his eyes on her shoulders and neck. Sometimes he would touch her secretly. He caressed her arm as she walked by or held her hand, hidden under a platter she was serving at the dinning-room table. In the nursery, when the boys were watching television, he would gently touch her lips with his fingers.

Leonora thought that if someone asked her what he was

like she would say he was like himself. If someone asked her what he smelled or tasted like she would say that he smelled and tasted like himself.

His breathing sounds like his own breath.

Two months later Leonora was positive that she was pregnant, and knew this meant that she would have to leave.

Drink new water.

Leonora told Mrs. O'Conner that she had to go back to her village, but Mrs O'Conner would not hear of it.

Mrs. O'Conner said, 'Don't be silly. This is nonsense. I cannot let you leave. My boys are attached to you. I need you now. You can't do this to me!'

'But my family needs me. My mother called . . .' Leonora answered.

'I'm sorry,' Mrs. O'Conner interrupted. 'You'll just have to tell your mother that I need you right now. Leonora, I cannot give you permission to leave. Not now and that is the end of it!'

I will let the rain fall. Let the river take the leaf. Let the wind move the leaf. Sweep the leaf.

Leonora hid her swelling body beneath aprons and large shirts until, four months later, Sofia finally noticed.

'Who did this to you?' Sofia demanded, touching Leonora's stomach. 'My God, Leonora what have you been up to? Who dropped coins into you?'

Leonora burst into tears, covered her eyes with her hands. 'I don't want to tell you,' she said.

'Well, you'd better tell me, since I am the only person who can help you.'

Leonora told Sofia the truth.

'You silly girl. Silly girl.' Sofia said, shaking her head back and forth. 'You are just an animal. You are a cow in the barn. What did you think was going to happen?'

Sofia told Leonora that she would have to tell Mr. O'Conner and that, if Leonora was lucky and the saints were on her side, he would take care of her and the baby.

'If you had only told me earlier,' Sofia said. 'There are ways to fix this right up with turpentine, or phosphorus scraped from the tips of the kitchen matches. I could have taken you to Moses. So, now I know, this is the air spirit in you!'

Aloe. Alum. Ammonia. Bitter apple. Borax. Camphor. Cotton root bark. Laburnum. Lead. Oil of thyme. Oleander leaves and bark. Quinine. Salts of arsenic. Slippery elm sticks. Yew.

'But I want this baby,' Leonora sobbed, 'It is mine. It is all I have. And I am not crying about the baby. I am crying because you know and then everyone will know. I did not want anyone to know.'

'Some women have tried to do it on their own with darning needles or even with umbrella ribs, but Moses knows how to do it so you are not hurt. But now it is too late. The baby is too big,' Sofia continued.

Before only God knew.

'You're so foolish. You are an animal, and nothing more,' Sofia said. 'But now that you are going to have a baby,' she continued with a sigh, 'there are a few things you need to know. It is a blessing, after all. We must never forget this.'

Before only God knew and protected me.

'Listen,' Sofia continued, 'do not tie an animal to a tree or your baby will be strangled with the umbilical cord. Wear broken scissors against your stomach so the baby will not have a defect. Sleep with stones on your chest so you will have good milk.'

Sleep with stones. Stones can bleed.

'Imagine,' Sofia continued, placing her arms around Leonora and holding her, 'just think, there are three of us in this room now. Three people, instead of two.'

Sofia rocked Leonora back and forth. 'Don't worry,' she continued. 'It will be a beautiful baby.'

I am two. There are two hearts, two livers and four kidneys inside of me. I have four legs and four arms. I have four eyes and two mouths.

A few days later Leonora was in the nursery with the boys when Mr. O'Conner came in. The boys were watching cartoons on the television, and Leonora was sitting on a chair by the door.

Run rabbit run. Fly bird fly.

Mr. O'Conner stood beside Leonora and rubbed her back and the nape of her neck. He put his fingers in his mouth and then rubbed his saliva behind her ear.

'Mr. O'Conner,' Leonora whispered. 'Shhh. I need to tell you this. I need to tell you. I thought I could leave. I did not want you to know. I tried to leave but Mrs. O'Conner said I had to stay. I have never learned to say "No". My mother taught me that it was a bad word. I need to tell you. Our baby is inside me.'

A spool of thread unwinding. The sound before rain.

'I'm sorry,' Mr. O'Conner answered, curling a strand of her hair around his finger. 'What did you say? Speak up.'

'Our baby is inside me,' Leonora whispered more loudly.

They part my garments among them.

Mr. O'Conner did not speak or move for a few seconds. He took his hand off of her neck and put it inside his pocket. She could hear his breath on her shoulders and smell the smell of himself.

'Leonora,' he said.

He said my name. Slap. Thunder. Butterfly.

'Leonora,' he said after a short pause. 'Everything will be fine. Don't worry. How far along are you?'

'Six months,' Leonora mouthed, without speaking.

Mr. O'Conner sighed and ran his fingers up along her arm.

He placed his hand on her belly.

Blessing. Blessing bark. Lead me in a plain path.

'We'll see,' he said. 'Be calm. You are the quietest woman I know. Don't make a fuss. Don't tell anyone. Don't tell Sofia.'

Leonora did not tell him that Sofia already knew since she did not want to make him angry. She was quite sure Josefa knew also because Sofia kept giving Leonora orange leaf tea with three spoons of honey in it, and telling her to go up to the roof and take a nap.

A few times a day Josefa looked straight at Leonora, clapped her hands together, and said, 'Tetanus.'

Everybody knows.

Twigs tearing. A green stick tearing. Slap. Thunder. Butter-fly. Crystal dove, glass dove, dove made from a window pane. I do not want to break you. I do not want to break you. Crystal dove I do not want you in pieces, broken on the floor.

Mr. O'Conner stood up and walked over to the boys.

He leaned over and kissed each of them and walked out of the room. Leonora heard him say, 'Oh sweet Jesus,' under his breath.

When the fly began to sing
Everyone was quiet,
It was a song
No one could hear.

EVERY LEAF IS A MOUTH

This is true: in hot weather, rain falls from lime trees.

Today, while I was having lunch, my left hand was calmly moving my fork from the plate to my mouth while my right hand kept picking up the salt shaker and shaking salt all over the floor. Sofia was telling me about ostriches. She said that they swallow glass, stones, and bricks to help them digest.

Once I finished shaking all the salt onto the floor, Leonora came in and swept it up. She says she likes to sweep because she likes brooms. I say, 'I know, I know.' Leonora kisses the top of my head and says, 'Happy birthday, birthday girl.'

It is December 12th.

Josefa walks in and says, 'Holes.'

Sofia says Josefa says this because, 'There are thirteen holes in your body.' We count them, but only count twelve.

Josefa says, 'Navel,' and we all laugh because we had forgotten about the navel.

'But the navel is closed,' I say.

'That was the hole for the umbilical cord,' Leonora explains. 'Where I come from we always bury the cord under a tree the day after the baby is born. The tree is grateful.'

Josefa says, 'Shape,' and not even Sofia knows what she means.

Josefa says it again, 'Shape,' and points to Leonora's large smallpox scar.

'Leonora has fourteen holes in her body,' Sofia says.

We all laugh.

Josefa's laugh sounds like short hiccoughs.

My mother does not like it when we sit around and talk. When she hears us laughing she storms into the kitchen. Leonora, Sofia and Josefa turn away from her and pretend to be working.

'What, for the love of God, is going on here?' my mother asks.

Everyone is silent. Nobody answers.

'Leonora,' my mother says, 'I asked you to clean the silver and you have not done it. I asked you to do it an hour ago! And Josefa, I want you to clean out all the rubbish bins. I don't think you have done that in two days! I am not paying any of you to sit around and talk!'

Everyone remains quiet, looking at the floor.

'And you!' my mother says pointing at me. 'It seems like you want to be a servant too, since you are in the kitchen all the time. Go to your room!'

When my mother walks out of the kitchen, Josefa, Leonora and Sofia start to giggle quietly.

Josefa says, 'Mustard.'

SOME THINGS WERE OVERHEARD AND SOME SAID IT WAS ALL A RUMOUR

One morning, a few days later, Leonora was upstairs on the roof washing clothes when she heard the sound of footsteps coming up behind her. She turned off the tap water and dried her hands on her apron. It was Mrs. O'Conner. She told Leonora that she wanted to speak to her.

Let the field be joyful, and all that is therein: then shall all the trees of the wood rejoice.

Mrs. O'Conner asked Leonora to come down to her bedroom. Leonora noticed that her face was swollen and her eyes were practically closed shut from crying. She looked blind.

'Yes, Mrs. O'Conner,' Leonora said, and followed her downstairs.

In the bedroom Mrs. O'Conner closed the door behind them and sat on the bed. She told Leonora that she knew everything. Mrs. O'Conner wept and rubbed her tears away with an embroidered, cotton handkerchief. She sucked on her diamond engagement ring.

Leonora could hear Mrs. O'Conner's thoughts. She was thinking, 'Ah. Crossed, crossed. Related, akin, coupled. What was it like? Where did she lie down?'

'The child will be raised in this house,' Mrs. O'Conner said. Leonora could hear her thinking, 'Ah. Five times? Six times? One year? Two years? Did it happen the day I was sick? Did it happen the day I went to Cuernavaca? Did it happen on those Saturdays I took the children to the park?'

Leonora's hands moved frantically as if she were knitting. She stepped back and answered Mrs. O'Conner's thoughts with her own.

He stepped on my shadow. I could not walk. And then I could not breath. I did not know what had happened until it happened. It was like trying to stop the rain. It was like holding a broom.

'It will be raised as if it were mine. I wish you had just left. Why didn't you run away? But you are not so noble are you?' Mrs. O'Conner continued. 'You can stay until it is nursed, and then you have to leave.'

'Yes,' Leonora said.

No.

'The child will be raised in this house and you will never tell anyone. You will not tell the child. You have to understand that it is best for the child. I told Mr. O'Conner that I wanted you to leave, but Mr. O'Conner says the child is his blood.'

'Yes,' Leonora said.

> *Let my cry come unto thee.*
> *. . . withered like grass; so that I forget to eat my bread.*

'Blood is thicker than water,' Mrs. O'Conner continued. Leonora could hear her thinking, 'Ah. White, black, good, bad, last, first. What is the name? The baptised name?'

Blood is thicker than milk, it turns hard in a few minutes. Blood becomes a stone.

'All I can promise you is that I will try to be kind to it. God knows it is innocent. All children are innocent, and then turn bad inside. And you were very bad, Leonora. Bad like a snake.'

Like an animal, like a cow in a barn. I am two. Two hearts, two mouths, two livers.

'Yes,' Leonora said.

I am a pelican of the wilderness.
I watch, and am as a sparrow alone upon the house top.

'For the love of God, how could you do this to my family?'
Mrs. O'Conner continued, sobbing harder. Leonora
could hear her thinking, 'Ah. There are not enough
rooms to fill this.'

Where I come from, there is only one room. There is one
room, and one life.

Mrs. O'Conner closed the curtains. Then she walked over
to the bed and slipped inside the covers. She still had her
clothes and shoes on. Leonora could hear her thinking,
'Ah. Ah. Ah.'

I have eaten ashes like bread.

'Get out and close the door behind you,' Mrs. O'Conner
said. 'And one more thing,' she continued. 'Tell me what
tricks did you use?'

'I'm sorry,' Leonora answered. 'I don't understand.'

'Yes,' Mrs. O'Conner said, 'Yes you do. I am not a fool.
I know that you servants use all kinds of Indian magic.

What did you do? Did you put your menstrual blood in his coffee? Did you put your hair and skin in his food? Did you put your nail parings in our bed? What trick did you use?'

'I learned at the convent never to do those things,' Leonora answered.

'Well, that is a silly answer, isn't it, Leonora,' Mrs. O'Conner answered sarcastically. 'What did you learn at the convent then? Certainly it wasn't the Ten Commandments.'

Leonora covered her face with her hands.

'I did learn them,' Leonora answered.

'When I insisted I only wanted a servant from a convent it was for a reason. I did not want my boys raised by an Indian, with all those Indian ideas. I wanted a girl who knew what was right and what was wrong!'

'Yes, Mrs. O'Conner,' Leonora said.

'And you have not even asked me to forgive you. You'd think I would deserve that,' Mrs. O'Conner continued in a whisper.

'I am sorry,' Leonora said.

'Don't answer back!' Mrs. O'Conner answered. 'I don't like the sound of your voice. You can leave now.'

Leonora slipped out of the room and closed the door behind her.

Sing unto him a new song; play skilfully with a loud noise.
My moisture is turned into the drought of summer.

EVERY LEAF IS A MOUTH

I'm really Leonora's teacher. Ever since kindergarten she has wanted to know everything that I am being taught. She's followed my education right at my side, and knows all about the atom bomb, the life cycle of plants, plate tectonics, the flora and fauna of Nigeria, and Mozart. When I tell her that we are the descendants of apes she laughs and tickles me. She says that is a lie, a cruel lie.

Even when I show her Darwin's book, she doesn't believe me.

Leonora says that everyone knows that people came from corn.

Sofia says she doesn't understand why Leonora wants to learn all those things that make your brain fat.

'Everything we need to know is in the wind and sky. If you look at things very closely, you'll find the answers,' Sofia says.

'This is true,' Leonora adds. 'Once I realised that a leaf

was just like a hand – with veins and everything. I knew then that trees were like people, only very quiet. And once, when there was a lot of wind, the tree was crying. I realised that the leaves were also mouths.'

'You don't have to learn the things that I'm studying, if you don't want to,' I say.

Leonora answers that she doesn't want to be separated from me by what I know. She says that she doesn't want there to be any walls between us.

'I'd hate it if you thought I was a stupid Indian,' she adds.

Sometimes, when Leonora and I are studying or doing homework, my father sits with us in the dining-room. He says Leonora is like an adopted daughter. She always closes her eyes when he says this.

He is very kind to her and strokes her hair and, sometimes, buys her chocolates. One Christmas he gave her a blue flannel nightgown. Leonora never wears it. She keeps it in her room in a box. She says she does not want it to get used up and worn out.

Sofia says that ever since my mother got the 'sleeping sickness' the house has been very quiet.

Josefa says, 'Somnambulant.'

As long as I can remember, my mother has been asleep most of the time. In her room the curtains are always closed. She even gets into bed with her clothes and shoes on. And even when she is awake she is yawning all the time.

Sofia says that this is because some people prefer sleep to being awake.

Josefa says, 'Dreams.'

'Yes,' Sofia says. 'Some people prefer their dreams to the living world.'

One night Leonora and I had the same dream. It was not exactly the same, but we both dreamed that we were in a forest.

This happened one morning when I was in the kitchen with Leonora, Josefa, and Sofia. Sofia was making caramel apples and the house was filled with the smell of boiling toffee.

I said, 'Last night I dreamt I was in a forest.'

'So did I,' Leonora said.

'I did too,' Sofia exclaimed.

Josefa said, 'Yes!'

We were all so surprised we began to laugh. Sofia said that actually it was not so remarkable since we all lived in the same house.

After this we used to tell each other our dreams all the time, but it never happened again.

Leonora said that this was because miracles can never be repeated.

'Miracles are always repeated,' Sofia answered. 'And having the same dream is hardly a miracle.'

'Coincidence,' Josefa said.

'Yes, it is a coincidence,' Sofia agreed.

'I like to believe in miracles,' Leonora said. 'If I don't, what is the point of living?'

'The point of living is figuring things out and knowing what is water and what is fire,' Sofia answered.

'You're mistaken,' Leonora said. 'The point of living is walking toward God and looking for Him.'

'You think you know everything because you lived at a convent,' Sofia said.

'That is not true and you know it,' Leonora said, smiling. 'Everything I know you taught me.'

Sofia walked over to Leonora and stroked her hair. Sofia loves Leonora. They are like a mother and daughter.

'Obedient,' Josefa said.

SOME THINGS WERE OVERHEARD AND
SOME SAID IT WAS ALL A RUMOUR

After Mrs. O'Conner had spoken to Leonora the house became very quiet. It was as if everyone was listening to Leonora's baby grow.

Mrs. O'Conner stopped going to work at the orphanage and she never went out in the evenings any more. It seemed as though she was afraid to leave the house. She slept all day or watched television and wore the same pink bathrobe all the time.

Mr. O'Conner was absent most of the time, but this had always been the case. When he did come home it was usually very late and he went straight to bed. On the weekends he would take the boys out for several hours, and then leave once again in the evening.

The three servants were mostly left to themselves. They took care of the house and the young boys.

When Leonora told Sofia and Josefa about her conversation with Mrs. O'Conner, Sofia said, 'Well, they are a good family. Servants have always had to give up their children or be put out on the street with their child.'

Josefa said, 'Corner.'

'The child will go to good schools and learn to read and write and maybe even go to university. This is the best way. They have been very good to you. Give thanks to God,' Sofia added.

Leonora wanted to bite a stick. She wanted to go upstairs and hit her arms and neck with the sticks that she kept under her bed.

'Muzzle,' Josefa said.

Mary, receive the flowers. Mary, receive the flowers that are so pure and beautiful, and with them my prayers, and with them my prayers.

'It has always been like this for servants,' Sofia continued. 'I remember a girl I once knew who worked for a family in Sonora. It was on a large cattle farm. The father and the son both used to go to her room, at different times, of course. The son would go there after school, and the father would sneak up to see her in the middle of the night. This went on for several years. Then she got pregnant and they threw her out. She ended up begging on the street with that baby tied to her back.'

81

'Tell me more,' Leonora said.

'Eleven,' Josefa answered.

'And then there was Concepcion.' Sofia added. 'I knew her very well. Her master began sleeping with her when she was thirteen, before she was really a woman. Men like to lie down with a virgin. When she was fifteen she got pregnant. She did everything she could to get rid of that child. She put small stones inside of her and punched her stomach with the back of a frying pan, but it did not work. She told me that she ran up and down stairs all the time and even slept with bricks on her stomach. The baby was born with eleven fingers. I'm sure this happened because of all that she had done to herself. The master said she was a whore since he would never have had a baby with eleven fingers.

'She left that house and I never saw her again. One of the other servants, who worked at that house as a cook, said she had tried to escape to the United States and that the border patrols caught her. Someone then said that they had seen her working in one of the border factories in Cuidad Juarez. They said she had changed her name from Concepcion to Lisa.'

'Jeans,' Josefa said.

'Yes,' Sofia answered. 'I think she works at a jeans factory.

Who knows what happened to the baby. It would be hard to love a baby with eleven fingers, but since I never had a baby I think I could love any child. They are angels, after all. Angels that are borrowed.'

'Sugar,' Josefa said.

'Yes,' Sofia answered. 'Like a cup of sugar.'

'Rice,' Josefa said.

Shew me thy ways, O lord; teach me thy paths.
The troubles of my heart are enlarged.

'Oh,' Sofia exclaimed, 'and how could I forget Matilde! She was very young, about fifteen also, like you, Leonora. She was working in a house with a very old couple. The man had been the head of the actor's union long ago and was now working with his son-in-law. When his wife discovered the truth, she threw Matilde out. Matilde ran to the man and hugged his legs and wept and told him to save her. She did this in front of the man's wife! But the man did not help her. For weeks Matilde spent all day outside that man's office waiting for him. When he arrived for work, or left in the evening, she was always there. He pretended he did not know her, even when she called out his name. He just ignored her and kept on walking.'

In the secret of his tabernacle shall he hide me;
he shall set me up upon a rock.

'Cut,' Josefa said.

'Yes. I heard that the man's wife divorced him,' Sofia added. 'You are lucky, Leonora, lucky that Mr. O'Conner believes that the baby is his.'

The baby is mine too. Broom-child. Tree child.

Leonora untied her braids and coiled her hair in a knot at the base of her neck.

I am a mother. A seed shall serve him.
I will wash my hands in innocency.

'One incredible story,' Sofia continued, 'happened to a French family. The young son fell in love with the servant and they used to spend every night together in her room. They were the same age. Then when he was about sixteen, he was sent away to school. While he was away there was a terrible accident and the servant accidentally burned her face. I think the stove exploded or something like that. The servant went back to her village. So, when the boy came back for the holidays, she was gone. When he was older he spent years trying to find her, but he never did.'

He hath put a new song in my mouth.

Leonora froze orange juice in ice cube trays and sucked on the cold cubes all day. She pulled grapefruits off the tree, sliced them up, and put them in her bathwater for good luck.

Every night at bedtime Sofia placed scissors on Leonora's stomach and stones on her breasts.

It moves in me. Does it weep in me? It feels like a broom, softly sweeping bread crumbs.

EVERY LEAF IS A MOUTH

Leonora says it's important to listen to your dreams because they are often filled with omens. She was taught this by her mother who learned about dreams from an old witch-doctor who had even taken care of Mexico's presidents and their families.

Leonora says that to dream of darkness is a bad sign; while to dream of light is a good sign. Tomatoes in a dream mean the lighted candles of a coming wake; guns mean the same candles, but not yet lighted. To dream of burning houses or corn fields indicates a coming fever. Snakes mean the ropes of a coffin. To dream of red things is bad; it means blood. If one dreams of loosing a tooth it means a child is going to die. To dream of vultures, black bulls, or horses is a sign of a funeral. To dream of young maize plants is a sign of rain.

Leonora asks me to promise not to forget this. She says I can be her teacher in school things, but that she is my teacher in the things that have to do with life.

When I tell this to Sofia she says that Leonora does not

know what she is talking about. Sofia thinks that we are all just like animals. Animals always pick on the weaker ones. She says my brother killed the ducks because they were weak.

Leonora says that in order to be strong I have to think of myself as strong, like a tall tree. I think I want to be a eucalyptus tree, but Leonora explains that is not a good tree because it has a very weak trunk for its size, and falls down easily in a big wind when it is old.

When my mother wakes up and sees me talking to Leonora, Josefa or Sofia in the kitchen she says I should not listen to their nonsense. She tells me to go to my room and stay there. Then, she goes back to her room and falls asleep. I wait fifteen minutes and then I go back down to the kitchen.

Once I told my mother a little bit about what Leonora had told me about dreams. I thought that it might be important for her to know since she sleeps all the time.

I said, 'Be careful if you dream about wolves because that means someone has placed the "Evil Eye" on you.'

My mother sat up in bed and stared at me.

'Who told you that?' She asked.

'Leonora,' I said. 'Leonora knows how to read dreams. Her mother taught her how.'

My mother told me to go and get Leonora.

When Leonora came into the bedroom, my mother stood up and slapped Leonora very hard across her cheek and began to yell at her, 'I never should have let you stay here! You are working against me! Indian! You are a witch!'

My father was outside in the garden and heard all the noise. He came upstairs. Leonora was crying and my mother was crying also.

'Stupid, silly women,' my father said as he walked into the room.

He told my mother to go back to bed. He told Leonora to go to her room.

'Stupid, silly women,' he said again.

Later he took me to the park and bought me some pistachio ice-cream. He told me that my mother and Leonora were idiots. He always calls my mother an idiot, even when he is being very nice to her. Sometimes he just calls her, 'Woman!', very slowly so it sounds like, 'Wooooomaaan!'

Leonora says that my father calls my mother an idiot because he loves her very much.

Josefa says, 'Stirrup.'

Sofia says that my father should hit my mother because it might wake her up. Sofia thinks that my mother needs to be hit just like you hit a mule that won't walk.

'If a man truly loves a woman he hits her,' Sofia explains.

The thought of my father hitting my mother makes me cry.

'Oh, don't cry,' Sofia says. 'Your father would never hit your mother. It is not in his nature. You cannot make a cat whistle, and you cannot make a dog fly.'

I wipe my tears with my right hand, while my left hand scratches my cheek.

Leonora comes over and sits beside me. She takes my right hand and says, 'Thine hand shall find out all thine enemies; thy right hand shall find out those that hate thee.'

'Oh, please!' Sofia says.

'Psalms,' Josefa adds.

Leonora learned these words at the convent.

She kisses my hand and whispers, 'Now know I that the Lord saveth his anointed; he will hear him from his holy heaven with the saving strength of his right hand.'

SOME THINGS WERE OVERHEARD AND
SOME SAID IT WAS ALL A RUMOUR

The baby girl was born on December 12th, the Day of the Virgin of Guadalupe.

The dark Virgin.

Mrs. O'Conner went with Leonora to the government clinic and stayed by her side during the birth. She held Leonora's hand, caressed her hair and cooled her face with a damp towel.

Leonora could hear her thinking, 'Ah. What will come? What will it be? Who will it be?'

Nothing hurts. The whole world is in me. O ye gates; even lift them up, ye everlasting doors.

Mrs. O'Conner rubbed Leonora's stomach and offered her sips of Coca-Cola to drink. 'You forget the pain later,' Mrs. O'Conner said. 'Once you see the baby you forget the pain.'

Pluck my feet out of the net.

Leonora could hear her thinking, 'Ah. Neglect, refuse, shun.'

When the baby girl was born Mrs. O'Conner said, 'Her name will be Aura Olivia.'

Leonora could hear her thinking, 'Ah. A name I can live with.'

The doctor placed the baby in Mrs. O'Conner's arms. She stared at the baby's face.

Leonora could hear Mrs. O'Conner thinking, 'There is no mirror here.'

Mrs. O'Conner placed the baby in Leonora's arms and went down to the clinic's offices and registered the child's birth as her own: Aura Olivia O'Conner Fuentes.

Alone in the room, Leonora held the baby and thought it smelled like fresh, new corn and sea salt. She could feel its small heart beat against her, fast like the heart of a bird or rabbit.

Try my reins and my heart.
My foot standeth in an even place.

Hearken O daughter, and consider,
And incline thine ear; forget also thine own people,
And thy father's house.

Twenty minutes later a priest came into the room. He was dressed in a black suit and had a gold crucifix hanging around his neck. He explained to Leonora that he was a priest who did services for the clinic and that Mrs. O'Conner had sent him to baptise the child.

Leonora gave him the baby. The priest carried the child over to the window and began to say some prayers. He took out a small bottle of water he was carrying in his pocket and dripped some of the liquid on the baby's head. After he had finished the baptising ritual, he slapped the baby's cheek hard. It made the baby cry. The priest turned to Leonora and said that he'd hit the child so it would remember the humility of Christ.

Stand with your head bowed to the sky. Kneel. Kiss the ground.

One day later, Leonora was back at the house with the baby. Sofia and Josefa had bought some flowers for her and some baby clothes. The three women sat on Sofia's bed and looked at the baby.

'Well, she looks just like you. I hope it is not a problem. Men like babies to look like them,' Sofia said.

Josefa said, 'Cathedral.'

Sofia said that one of the baby's hands looked like a maple leaf, while the other one looked like a pine cone.

Broom-child. Good morning dark dove, today I come to greet you, greeting your beauty in your celestial reign.

Leonora gave Sofia and Josefa a plastic bag with the baby's umbilical cord inside of it. This was so that they could bury it in the garden under the large grape-fruit tree.

'It is good that you remembered,' Sofia said.

'Memory,' Josefa said.

'The doctor did not want to give it to me. He said it was Indian witchcraft, but I insisted,' Leonora said.

'Remember,' Josefa said.

Mrs. O'Conner told Leonora that she could keep the baby in her room at night for the first three months while she breastfed. Then, Mrs. O'Conner explained, the baby would be moved to the nursery downstairs.

'Think of yourself as a wet nurse,' Mrs. O'Conner had

said. 'You would be a very silly girl if you start to get sentimental about all of this. Remember she is my child and Mr. O'Conner's child.'

'Yes, Mrs. O'Conner,' Leonora had answered.

'In a few months we will let people know that we have adopted a child and then that will be the end of it all. Then you can start looking for a new job, just as we agreed.'

'Yes, Mrs. O'Conner,' Leonora had replied.

I want to remember all the songs I know.

Two weeks after Aura was born, Leonora was on the roof washing clothes. She had placed Aura in the garden on a blanket. From the roof, Leonora saw Mr. O'Conner walk out into the garden and stand above the baby. He looked down at her for ten minutes. Then he knelt beside the baby and slowly caressed her cheek with his finger.

After a few minutes Mrs. O'Conner walked out into the garden. When she saw her husband with the baby she walked over to him. Mr. O'Conner got up off his knees and they both stood together, their heads bowed, staring at the child.

Leonora could hear Mrs. O'Conner's thoughts. They

moved out of the garden, up the walls to the roof, and into her ears.

Mrs. O'Conner was thinking, 'He does not move away. He has accepted everything. He does not see what he has done to me.'

Women at the river, beating stones, washing against stones. Hearts beat against stones. The fabric bleeds in the water. Blue, blue, orange, red in the river. The heart bleeds in the river. Rag and blouse, rag and stone beat in the river.

The next day Mrs. O'Conner said that Leonora had to start looking for a new job or go back to her village.

Arms in the river. Braids in the river.

'You have to leave sooner than I had anticipated. You simply cannot stay here,' Mrs. O'Conner said. 'It will be the best for everyone. The sooner you leave the better. Maybe you can go back to your village for some time and rest and see your family.'

'Yes,' Leonora answered.

'I know I told you you could stay for a while, but now I realise that that was a mistake,' Mrs. O'Conner continued.

In the evening, Leonora told Sofia what Mrs. O'Conner had said.

'If I have to leave I am taking the child with me. I don't care what I promised. Everything seems different now. The baby came out of my skin,' Leonora explained with large tears forming in her eyes.

Sofia said, 'You cannot do that! The child is not registered in your name. Don't you see!'

'But she is mine! She came out of me! She grew in me!' Leonora protested.

'The law is the law,' Sofia said. 'Her name is O'Conner Fuentes and the law only thinks about that!'

'But in her blood she is me. I will do what I have to do. Mrs. O'Conner promised I could stay and now she says I have to leave!' Leonora said.

'Not only *your* blood,' Sofia answered. 'Listen. They will never call your child a bastard. I am a bastard and so are you, and so are all your grandmothers!'

Give ear to my prayer.

'When I think of my childhood I know what can happen,'

Sofia continued. 'I was sent to work with a family when I was only eight years old. They only gave me half a glass of milk and a piece of bread to eat. There was a parrot in a cage in the kitchen and it was fed more than I was. I used to spend all day waiting for the moment I could steal food from that cage. I ate the parrot's pieces of banana, orange and, if it was early in the morning, I could even steal some of its peanuts before they were finished. No food ever tasted more delicious than that parrot's food.'

A few days later, while Sofia was making coffee and breakfast, Mr. O'Conner came into the kitchen.

'I have to speak to you, sir,' she said. 'Something might happen and I have to tell you.'

'Yes. What is it, Sofia?' Mr. O'Conner asked.

'I do not want Leonora to get into trouble,' Sofia said and proceeded to tell him that Leonora was planning to run away with the baby. 'Mrs. O'Conner has asked her to leave immediately,' Sofia explained in a quick rush of words. 'She changed her mind and now Leonora thinks she can leave with the baby. I've told her not to do this, but she won't listen to me. I told her it would make you very angry. I told her the baby has a future here. Leonora thinks she can feed that baby with love. Leonora is only sixteen years old! She doesn't understand the world.'

'You did the right thing,' Mr. O'Conner answered quietly. 'Thank you, Sofia. You have always been very loyal to our family. I appreciate this very much.'

Later that afternoon, Mr. O'Conner went outside to the garden where Leonora was sweeping dry leaves off of the grass. He stepped on Leonora's shadow. Leonora held the broom against her chest like a body.

My heart is a leaf on the ground.

'You are not leaving,' Mr. O'Conner told her. 'You will stay here with the child.' He kissed her on the mouth and caressed her hair. 'You are a mother now. You have to think differently. You are the silent mother, but the important mother, and you know how to keep quiet.'

He kissed her again, deep into her mouth.

Hummingbird.

Harvest.

He drew her against him, pushed her toward the grapefruit tree, and lifted up her apron and skirt. The wooden broomstick was like a rib between them. He caressed her and slipped a finger deep inside of her.

Can you keep a secret? No one is looking?

'Listen, Leonora,' Mr. O'Conner said, 'my child is not going to end up looking for twigs in the forest. I won't allow that.'

He kissed her neck.

'If you take the child away, I will put you in jail.'

He kissed her mouth.

'Be a good mother,' he continued. 'Be the best mother of all.'

Like an animal, like a cow in a barn.

He kissed her arm.

'You don't want to go to jail, do you?' he asked.

> *Thou tellest my wanderings: put thou*
> *My tears into thy bottle: are they not in*
> *Thy book?*

Leonora shook her head.

'So, be good,' he said.

Attend unto me, and hear me: I mourn in my complaint, and make a noise.

'So, be good,' he said again. 'I'll take care of Mrs. O'Conner and tell her to leave you alone.'

Timorous body why get frightened? Cowardly body, don't be afraid. I stretch out my arms. There is a cross in me. Drink. Swallow the river and clouds. I can taste the day I was born.

That night, before going to sleep, Leonora told Sofia that Mr. O'Conner had spoken to her and told her that if she took the baby away she would go to jail.

'That is exactly what I told you,' Sofia said as they lay in the dark. 'The baby has a name, a family name and a father's name. They have been very kind to you.'

'But what will the baby think? She only looks like me. Don't you think she'll know?' Leonora asked.

'The baby will never know,' Sofia said. 'And don't you ever tell her. That child will hate you if you tell her. If you really love the baby, you know that this is for the best. These things have been happening for hundreds of years. Men have always had children where they are not supposed to. If you want that child to love you, don't ever say a word!'

I am a mirror. A Secret. The best mother.

EVERY LEAF IS A MOUTH

My father is always telling my mother that the house is not clean. He wipes his fingers behind curtains, over door knobs, and on the window sills.

'Your mother never does what she is supposed to do,' he says.

He asks her if she has brushed her teeth, if she has taken his suit to the tailor, if she has bought bread, and complains that she sleeps too much. He whispers these things to her in a deep voice. He walks past her and murmurs, 'There is hair in the sink.'

My father tells my mother that she forgot the bread, she forgot to buy lemons, and that she forgot to pay the telephone bill. He likes to tell her about everything she has forgotten. He tells her she is getting fat and that she is too thin. He tells her to go bathe.

Every time he tells my mother these things she closes her eyes. Her eyelids are like a wall, when she closes them no one can talk to her anymore. She closes her eyes and stumbles to her bedroom, holding onto tables, chairs, and walls as she walks. It's as if she were blind.

Sofia says that my father is a nag.

'Usually it's the woman who badgers,' Sofia explains. 'But here it is the other way around. Of course no one denies that she sleeps too much. It's an illness. You wouldn't be cruel to someone if they were missing a leg, would you?'

Leonora is very kind to my mother and always helps her. Leonora holds my mother's arms and walks her back to the bedroom, slips off her shoes, helps her get in bed, and gives her some tea made from the leaves of the grapefruit tree.

Sometimes Leonora sings my mother songs like the song about the deer, 'Look out, or you will crush me Big Deer. Go away, for I got here before you did.' Or, 'If you take me with you, I shall tell you, I shall tell you who is eating your cornfield.'

When I was about eight years old my mother began to buy fish for the stray cats in the neighbourhood. Soon we had at least nineteen cats living in our house and garden. My mother loved these cats and had names for all of them. After a while she could not think of anymore names so she called them, 'One, Two, Three, Four, Five,' and on and on. Sofia said that it was the Christian thing to do because every creature deserved a name.

One night, after we had all gone to sleep, my father scattered some meat around the garden. The meat was filled with rat poison. The next morning all the cats were gone.

The following day, Leonora told us the whole story. She said that she was fast asleep in her room on the roof when she heard a soft knocking sound on the door. It was my father. He told her to get her plastic gloves, several garbage bags, and go downstairs and help him clean up the mess in the garden.

Leonora says that my father had a flashlight with him, even though there was a moon, and the garden was brightly lit by the street lights. She explained that it took about an hour to pick up all those cats, and that their bodies were still warm.

'Even through the plastic gloves I could feel the heat,' Leonora said, rubbing her hands up and down her apron.

My mother never really knew what had happened, and she never brought it up. I think she suspected that my father must have done something since, from then on, she always said, 'THE CATS' to him. She would say things like, 'Good morning, THE CATS,' or 'The plumber called, THE CATS.'

Leonora said that it was a terrible thing to do. She said she was always protecting my mother from things that were killed, like the ducks Francisco hung from the tree.

'I have had to pick up too many dead things,' Leonora said. 'I was not made for this. It was not in God's plans for me. My hands were made for gathering twigs and weeds, and not for touching blood.'

Sofia asked, 'How many cats were there?'

Leonora answered, 'At least thirty.'

'Thirty. That's not so bad. I thought there were more than that. Still, it must have been awful,' Sofia said.

'The worst of it was picking up the kittens,' Leonora added.

Josefa said, 'Candles.'

'We can't light thirty candles,' Sofia said. 'I think we only have four.'

'I know,' I answered. 'You can light one big one for all of them.'

Josefa clapped her hands.

Sofia rubbed my cheek and said I was very intelligent. Then she went to the dinning-room and brought back one candle and lit it from the stove burner.

'May God and all the Saints forgive Mr. O'Conner,' Sofia prayed.

'Tails,' Josefa said.

'Amen,' Leonora said.

'And,' Sofia added, 'may we all live to see a light that is greater than the sun and all the stars.'

'Heads,' Josefa said.

SOME THINGS WERE OVERHEARD AND
SOME SAID IT WAS ALL A RUMOUR

One afternoon while Sofia and Leonora were sitting in the kitchen polishing the silver, Sofia said, 'A lifetime and a house are always marked by events. This house is marked by many things. Just look at these spoons,' she continued, picking up a serving spoon. 'Imagine everything that has happened while they were being used. I often think that voices are embedded in everything.'

The rings on a tree. Circles around the tree trunk. Hoops, bands. Wedding rings.

'I tell myself,' Sofia continued, 'that the marks on this house are very clear. Before you came, Mr. O'Conner had a mistress. Then Mrs. O'Conner found out that he had even known the woman before they were married. And, he has had many women, just like his father did. Mrs. O'Conner even found out that he had called his mistress from the hospital when Francisco was born. Mrs. O'Conner once told me about this, and called her life a big, fat lie. She said that he had stolen her life and that he was a robber. Then she just tried to live for the church, and the orphanage, and her boys. I say you can be too much of a Catholic. Then Aura was born. Then Francisco killed the ducks and hurt the house with that blood. And then Mr. O'Conner killed all those cats . . .'

How can anyone walk in the garden. The garden of dead cats. He held my arm and told me I could do it. He said I could do it because I had an Indian heart and my hands were strong. I am not so strong, but stronger than I thought.

'I told Mrs. O'Conner that her life was not so bad. I said that there were people who were hungry and hurt and that she was warm and whole,' Sofia continued. 'You always have to measure your grief against someone else's, because there is bound to be someone who is in more trouble than you are.'

'You are so good with words,' Leonora answered. 'You always seem to know what to say about everything.'

'Mrs. O'Conner said that I was right. She is not a stupid woman. She knows that most women don't really mind much, but she cannot stand it. It makes her feel contaminated. This is why she sleeps so much, to try and get clean . . . what I mean is to get her mind clean, of course.'

Meet me at the river.

'If she really wanted help, I could have helped her. She is too much of a Catholic, and so I never even mentioned it,' Sofia continued. 'She should have put her tears in his tea or coffee, and that would have solved everything. No man can stand to drink his wife's tears.'

'Can anyone do that?' Leonora asked.

'Well,' Sofia answered. 'It only works if you're married. I knew a woman once who used to peel an onion until she cried. Then, she let her tears fall into a glass of water. She did this every night. Her husband always drank that glass of water before he fell asleep. He always loved her. It worked.'

'If Josefa were here she would say, "salt"' Leonora said laughing.

'No,' Sofia answered with a smile. 'If Josefa were here she would have said, "onion" because she'd be thinking about trying this magic out immediately! She knows a lot more about these tricks than I do. But she's very secretive.'

After they had finished polishing the silver, Leonora and Sofia went out to the garden and sat under the grapefruit tree. It was beginning to get dark and they could hear the distant sound of the whistle that belonged to a man who sold steamed yams from a cart.

'Now I am getting too old ...' Sofia said, picking up a grapefruit from the ground and peeling it with her fingers. 'It is time for me to leave. I don't know if I am a mark here or not. I have worked for this family my whole life and I will leave here with nothing. The O'Conners will give me a year's wages and that will be that, after almost forty years of working for them. I have buried them and seen them born.'

'But you cannot leave me,' Leonora said. 'I'll go with you. We can live together somewhere.'

'You'll never leave Aura Olivia. You'll never leave your child. You'll serve the guests at her wedding,' Sofia answered.

Obey. Touch my shoulder. No one will look at my back. No one will see the back of my arms and neck walking away. No one will hear me close the door and my steps walking down the street.

Leonora knew she was right. She would never leave. She needed to teach Aura all the songs she knew.

I sing that I may be heard, not because my voice is good.

Let their eyes not see me, let their feet not reach me, may their hands not touch me. I sing that I may be heard.

After Aura was born Leonora never went back to her village to see her family. Sometimes her mother would call and beg her to come home for a visit, but Leonora never did. She was afraid that if she ever left the house she might find that the O'Conner's had changed the locks on the doors and that she could not get back inside. She even stopped going out on her day off.

Leonora imagined what would happen if she left. She could see herself standing on the street for hours frantically knocking on the door, and ringing the doorbell.

No answer.

Let me in. Let me in. Let me in.

EVERY LEAF IS A MOUTH

'This is a house of women,' Sofia says, because now my brothers have gone away to boarding school, and my father travels all the time. 'Who would ever have thought that this house would become a hen pen?'

Leonora explains that living with women reminds her of the time she used to live at a convent. 'My arms feel very warm,' she says. 'They always used to feel warm at the convent.'

'The moon is very kind to a house of women,' Sofia adds.

Josefa says, 'Craters.'

I have always liked to spend time in the kitchen or on the roof with Leonora, Sofia, and Josefa, but now sometimes my mother comes also.

'I think she is lonely,' Leonora says.

'No,' Sofia answers. 'She just wants company.'

'What is the difference?' Leonora asks.

'She isn't lonely. It is the moon that pulls us all together just like it pulls the oceans,' Sofia explains.

Some afternoons when Sofia, Josefa, Leonora and I are up in the servants' room on the roof watching our favourite soap opera my mother will come up and sit with us. Everyone moves around to give her some space on Leonora's bed.

Josefa likes the commercials. She hops up and down when the commercial for Coca-Cola comes on. This commercial shows two people dancing. I think that Josefa must see four people dancing. I am always wondering what she sees. Josefa likes the music, but cannot dance. She hops instead, and makes us all laugh. Even my mother laughs.

We are all amazed at my mother because she always knows exactly what is going to happen in the soap opera. We beg her not to tell us, but she cannot help herself. While we are watching she says, 'That woman is going to be in a car crash,' or, 'That man is really a priest in disguise,' or, 'Mark my words, she is not his sister; she is his mother.'

Sofia greatly respects her because of this, and wonders if my mother might be clairvoyant.

In one of these soap operas there is a woman who keeps a diary. Everything the character writes down is then acted out. This makes Leonora very excited. She says that she would love to be able to write down everything that she thinks about.

Sofia says, 'You know how to write, so what is stopping you?'

Leonora answers, 'I just cannot imagine how to do it. How do you get what you are thinking out of yourself?'

'I'll help you,' I said.

One morning I went into the kitchen with three sheets of paper and a pen. I told Leonora I was going to show her how easy it was, and asked her to dictate all her thoughts to me.

She leaned against the stove and closed her eyes. After a little while she said, 'I was born.'

I wrote this down.

'My mother tied plastic bags around my feet to keep them warm in the winter.'

I wrote this down.

'I have never liked to eat meat,' Leonora continued. 'Because I can always see the animal's eyes.'

I wrote this down.

'My favourite colour is blue,' Leonora added. 'My favourite number is five. My favourite day of the week is Wednesday.'

I wrote this down, but then Leonora opened her eyes and said, 'This is impossible, if I speak what I am thinking then it is not a thought any more!'

Sofia says that Leonora is very stubborn. 'You'd think sometimes that she's a cousin of the mule,' she says.

Yesterday my father came home unexpectedly after being away for three weeks. He says that he is helping a banker who stole a lot of money from the government and is hiding in Costa Rica. I ask my father why he wants to help a thief, and he explains that lawyers must do these things.

The story about the banker is in all the newspapers and on the television news. Every morning Sofia spreads out the newspaper on the kitchen table and we all read about it. Sofia even cuts out the pictures of my father at the courthouse and hangs them up in her bedroom beside her altar to the Virgin of Guadalupe. She has been doing this for years. There are newspaper clippings of my parents on her walls from even before the time I was born. Some have yellowed and begun to crack.

Sofia says that what my father is doing is just like selling your soul. She wants to know if you would cut off your hand for one million pesos.

My mother sighs and tells Sofia that she does not understand anything, and explains that everyone, even the worst criminal, has a right to be defended.

Sofia says she expects us all to be defended in heaven, because this is God's job and not a human job. She says, 'Think about all the food that man in Costa Rica stole from my mouth!'

Leonora says that even the most crooked tree has a wooden cross inside of it.

Josefa says, 'Glass,' and keeps her crossed-eyes shut for a long time.

I wonder what Josefa sees when she closes her eyes. When I close my eyes I see a black sky. When Josefa closes her eyes perhaps she sees two black skies.

Once I even asked her.

She closed her eyes for a very long time, as if she were trying to figure it out. I could see her eyeballs moving around in circles under her eyelids.

She said, 'Egg.'

SOME THINGS WERE OVERHEARD AND
SOME SAID IT WAS ALL A RUMOUR

Mrs. O'Conner sleeps most of the morning and, sometimes, in the afternoon, she goes up to the servants' quarters on the roof to watch soap operas. She walks up the stairs quietly and sits on the bed with Leonora, Sofia, Josefa, and Aura. Sometimes she brings a large bag of peanuts or candies for everyone.

The four women and one girl sit together in a crowded heap on Sofia's bed. Their feet touch. They lean into and away from each other. Sometimes Leonora brushes Mrs. O'Conner's hair or rubs cream on her arms.

A broomstick
can be a body
to embrace.

One day Aura was away at a friend's house, Sofia was in the kitchen making hominy soup with radishes and oregano, and Josefa had not come to work. Leonora was alone in her room on the roof hemming some linen napkins when she heard Mrs. O'Conner's steps coming up the stairs, a pitter-patter of soft bedroom slippers.

Mrs. O'Conner sat beside Leonora on the bed and watched her stitch for a few minutes, moving the needle in and out in fast, short movements.

'You do that beautifully. I never learned how to sew properly. I never had the patience,' Mrs. O'Conner said.

'Thank you,' Leonora answered. 'The nuns were good teachers.'

Then Mrs. O'Conner leaned over and took the needle out of Leonora's hand. She stretched her arms above her head and yawned.

'It is not the infidelities that hurt so much and break your heart,' Mrs. O'Conner said. 'It's that all those women's cells get into your body. They move around in you, like fish. They swim inside and make you forget who you are. You eat things you don't like. Yesterday I ate some marshmallows. I hate marshmallows! Then I find I am wearing clothes I don't even like. It is better to sleep and be calm.'

Leonora gently rubbed Mrs. O'Conner's hand. Mrs. O'Conner quickly moved her hand away and began to poke at her palm with the needle, but without breaking the skin.

They that sit in the gate speak against me; and I was the song of the drunkards.

119

'You might think that I'm stupid. Mr. O'Conner thinks I am stupid, but I am positive that there is scientific proof,' Mrs. O'Conner continued. 'You are in me Leonora. Just think how it works: He kisses you and then he kisses me. He carries you into me. I never wanted to have you in me. I never asked for this. Who knows how many women are in me, and now a servant is in me. A servant and your Indian blood! Even the thoughts of these women come into my mind. It frightens me. I know their voices. One says, "Call me," and another says, "At four, my darling." I could almost stand this. But then it happened with you. How can I even stand up straight when my husband has slept with my servant?'

Leonora gently took the needle out of Mrs. O'Conner's hand.

'Your voice is different from the other women's voices. Isn't that strange? At first I heard it like a scratch or a scrape in me. But now it is such a beautiful voice. It is like humming, a soft, sweet hum. And I wonder how can a voice be so lovely?'

The plowers plowed upon my back;
They made long their furrows.

'Why is your voice so sweet and soothing,' Mrs. O'Conner asked, 'like a delicate song?'

Leonora picked up her hair brush and began to brush Mrs. O'Conner's hair. This was something she had done frequently and it had always soothed Mrs. O'Conner. Ever since Aura was born, Leonora instinctively knew that she had to be very kind and careful. She even grew to enjoy taking care of Mrs. O'Conner. She thought that it was like taking care of a beautiful altar at a church.

'Don't!' Mrs. O'Conner said, moving away from her and over to Sofia's bed. 'That brush has your hair in it. Your hair will be mixed with my hair!'

'Yes, Mrs. O'Conner,' Leonora said, putting the brush down and folding her hands together on her lap.

Lift up your hands in the sanctuary.

Mrs. O'Conner turned toward Leonora's bedside table and picked up a photograph of Aura taken on the day of her birth. The nurses at the clinic had given it to Leonora and now it lay on the table beside a postcard of the Virgin of Guadalupe, and a clay bowl filled with hair clips and dry, brown lemons.

'I can give you more photographs, if you like,' Mrs. O'Conner said. 'You can look through the family photograph albums and take any you might like.'

Leonora knew the photographs well: Aura with the boys

in Chapultepec Park; Aura skiing beside her father; Aura on her first day of school; Aura with Mickey Mouse at Disneyland; Aura at her First Communion; Aura with her broken arm; Aura sitting on the steps of the house . . .

'Yes, yes, thank you, Mrs. O'Conner,' Leonora answered.

'Leonora,' Mrs. O'Conner continued, 'It is time. You know what I mean. You were never supposed to stay here as long as you have, you know this. The time has come for you to leave.'

That our daughters may be
as corner stones,
polished after the similitude of a palace.

Leonora could hear Mrs. O'Conner thinking, 'I will help you pack. I will help you fold. Ah. I will give you my suitcase.'

Rid me, and deliver me from the hand
of strange children,
whose mouth speaketh vanity,
and their right hand
is a right hand of falsehood.

'The years go by and by and you are still here,' Mrs. O'Conner continued. 'I still remember the day I picked you up at the convent. You were so young and pretty, and so eager to please me.'

Leonora also remembered that day when Mrs. O'Conner had picked her up at the convent. She could still smell the clean, leather seats of the car mixed with Mrs. O'Conner's perfume of apricots, which filled the air and made her feel serene. She remembered how she had stared at Mrs. O'Conner's hands with their perfectly groomed fingernails.

'And I thought you were so lovely with your long arms and fingers. I even told Mr. O'Conner that I had found the perfect girl, and he agreed,' Mrs. O'Conner said.

Leonora looked down at the ground and covered her face with one hand.

'You were so good to the boys and you learned everything so quickly. No one irons as well as you do. Mr. O'Conner even said that you were the best kind of servant because you seemed invisible. We did not even feel your presence. But you were a spider!'

A wishing well. Charm. Talisman. Amulet.

'Please don't make me have to throw you out,' Mrs. O'Conner said. 'It is better for everyone if you accept this.'

Leonora could hear Mrs. O'Conner thinking, 'Ah. Animal. Indian. Sister.'

Mrs. O'Conner continued, 'The church needs someone, a caretaker, should I tell them you can go there? Or maybe you can go back to your village. You understand, of course, that I cannot possibly recommend you to any of our friends.'

Leonora could hear Mrs. O'Conner thinking, 'And I might learn to wake up.'

> *Remember the song:*
> *One child fell in the wishing well*
> *and then they covered it up.*
> *The child drowned in the wishing well*
> *and then they covered it up.*
> *They covered it up with stones and boards,*
> *with stones and boards,*
> *with stones and boards,*
> *but the child still cries*
> *and weeps for home.*

'You have one month,' Mrs. O'Conner said, standing up and walking toward the door. 'I have already talked this over with Mr. O'Conner, and he agrees completely.'

The grapefruits fall from the tree like stones.

EVERY LEAF IS A MOUTH

One afternoon the police came to our house. My father was not home since he had been in Costa Rica for the past three weeks. My mother, Leonora, Sofia, Josefa and I were watching television upstairs in the servants' room when we heard the doorbell ring several times, followed by a loud bang on the front door and the sound of a dog barking.

Josefa cried, 'Zoo!' and jumped up and ran downstairs.

Sofia turned off the television and said, 'This is more noise than the noise the man makes who comes once a month to sharpen the knives.'

My mother yawned and covered her mouth.

Josefa returned a few minutes later and said, 'Tamarind.'

My mother stood up and rubbed her eyes. 'So soon,' she said. 'It seems so soon.'

We all went downstairs and my mother opened the door.

Standing in the doorway were three policemen. One of the policemen, who wore dark sunglasses, held a large dog on a worn leather leash.

My mother ushered them into the living-room, while Sofia, Leonora, Josefa and I were told to go and wait in the kitchen.

Sofia said, 'And what, I ask myself in the name of the sweet Virgin, does this mean?'

Josefa said, 'Persevere.'

The four of us sat around the kitchen table and tried to listen to the muffled sound of the voices coming from the living-room. Sofia picked at her gold teeth with her thumbnail, while Leonora twirled her hair around one of her fingers. My right hand curled up into a fist.

After fifteen minutes, my mother came in and told Josefa, Leonora, and Sofia that the policemen wanted to talk to them and to please follow her to the living-room. She told me to go to my room. Sofia, Leonora, and Josefa looked frightened. Josefa began to hiccough.

I went upstairs to my room and sat beside the door trying to listen to what was happening downstairs. After a short time, I heard soft cries and a voice, which sounded like Sofia, saying, 'This is not the way to take care of things.'

Then I heard the sound of the policemen walking up to the servants' quarters with the dog. It seemed to make the whole house shake to have all those men walking around on the roof. I also heard Leonora saying something that sounded like, 'Ohnoonnoonno.'

After a short while, I heard the policemen go back down again to the living-room. Someone was crying. It sounded like my mother. One of the policemen kept saying, 'Pleasure'. A few minutes later the policemen walked out the front door and drove away. Then everything was very quiet as if everyone were holding their breath.

A few minutes later my mother came up to my room and told me what had happened. She said her diamond engagement ring had been missing for a week, and that the policemen had found it under Leonora's pillow. The policemen had taken Leonora to jail.

I remember that this happened once in one of the soap operas we used to watch. In the soap opera, though, the servant had stolen the family's silver. She had stolen it to save her brothers who were in jail. That soap opera was called, 'Heaven on Earth'; and none of us liked it very much.

When I went up to Leonora and Sofia's room later in the day, Sofia and Josefa were sitting on Leonora's bed. Everything in the room was turned upside down and there were muddy paw prints from the police dog all over Leonora's bed. Sofia was crying and Josefa was saying, 'Rabbit' over and over again. The room had a lingering smell of men's cologne.

When Sofia saw me she stretched out her arms and drew me to her. She stroked my hair and said, 'This is a very bad day.'

'Rabbit,' Josefa said.

'But why would she steal?' I asked. It was hard for me to imagine Leonora taking anything that did not belong to her.

'Do you think she stole?' Sofia answered. 'Do you think her soul is made of rags?'

'Rabbit,' Josefa said.

'I wish your father were here,' Sofia said. 'He would fix this up. He never would have called the police. He never would have allowed this to happen.'

My left arm began to move in the air; hingeless.

'Snake,' Josefa said.

Sofia reached out and caught my arm, and held it tight against her stomach.

'I'll find your father as soon as I can,' Sofia said. 'I'll call his secretary in the morning. I don't care if Mrs. O'Conner gets angry or not.'

'Run,' Josefa said.

Later in the evening, when I was getting ready for bed, my mother came in to my room to say goodnight. Her eyes were swollen and her face was pale from crying.

'This is a bad day,' she said holding my hands.

'That is just what Sofia said,' I answered.

'She did?' my mother asked.

'Yes,' I replied. 'Sofia said that it was a bad day. And Josefa said that my arm was moving like a snake.'

'Did Josefa say anything else?' my mother asked.

'Of course,' I answered. 'She said "Rabbit".'

My mother lay down beside me on the bed. She held me

in her arms and rubbed my back. 'What have I done?' she sobbed.

'You did the right thing,' I said. 'She shouldn't have stolen the ring that Daddy gave to you? That was very bad.'

'Oh, little Fly,' my mother said.

She had never called me Fly before. I guess it just came out.

It's only a word.

Fly.

SOME THINGS WERE OVERHEARD AND
SOME SAID IT WAS ALL A RUMOUR

In the police car Leonora's wrists were loose inside the handcuffs. She could easily have slipped her hands out. One of the policemen and the dog were in the back seat beside her. They had placed a muzzle over the dog's mouth before leading it into the car. Leonora leaned her body against the car door and pressed her face against the window.

Do not make anyone angry.

Since it was the first time that Leonora had left the house in so many years, she felt as if she were looking at the world for the first time. This sensation reminded her of the first time she had driven into Mexico City in Mrs. O'Conner's car.

The policemen mostly ignored her as they drove to the station. They talked about a recent bullfight where the matador had been badly gored.

'That bull was given some kind of drug,' the policeman in the back seat, beside Leonora, said.

131

The other policemen agreed.

'It was probably injected with speed,' the policeman continued. 'Bulls don't act like that. You could see that something was very wrong when that animal ran into the ring. It was fucking crazy!'

'Yes,' the policeman who was driving answered. 'Or maybe they injured it badly before they let it run out . . . an electric shock on its leg or something.'

'Or maybe it was jealous,' the policeman in the front seat beside the driver added.

'A bull can always smell sex!' the driver said laughing.

The policeman who was sitting beside Leonora turned to her and asked, 'Do you like the bullfights?'

Leonora, not answering, looked down at her hands that were locked in the cold metal.

'You're a pretty one,' the policeman continued. 'You look just like my sister. You have nice white teeth. I bet they gave you good food at that house.'

Leonora did not answer.

And of thy mercy cut off mine enemies, and destroy all of them that afflict my soul: for I am thy servant.

'Cat's got your tongue? Huh?' he asked. 'Why did you steal from that pretty lady's house?'

'No, sir,' Leonora said, without lifting up her eyes to look at him. 'I did not take anything.'

'Leave the poor thing alone,' the policeman who was driving said, and everyone was quiet. 'I'm feeling hungry,' he added after a little while, 'Let's go and get something to eat.'

The policeman stopped the car in front of a small restaurant that had tables outside on the sidewalk.

'We'll have to leave you here,' the driver said to Leonora. 'We cannot have our prisoner sitting at the table with those manacles on. We'd have to feed you like a baby!'

The other policemen laughed.

They left Leonora in the car with the dog while they ate and drank beer. Every now and then one of the policemen would walk over to the car and check on her.

Leonora knew what the policemen meant when they said that the bull had been jealous. In her village everyone knew that you never hunt an animal after having sex, because the animal will get jealous.

> *Before he takes his bow, his spear, his arrows,*
> *he will not touch me,*
> *fearing to make them jealous:*
> *the jaguar, the monkey, the deer.*
> *I too am like the animals,*
> *when he hunts I cry.*

She slipped her hands out of the handcuffs and sucked on her fingers.

When the policemen came back to the car she carefully slipped them back inside.

She did not want to make them angry.

She did not want them to see her.

She did not want them to know she was alive.

EVERY LEAF IS A MOUTH

Sofia knows everything.

Sofia says that she knows too many people that have gone to jail for no good reason, and that the really bad people never get caught.

'That is Mexico!' she says.

Two days after Leonora was put in jail, Josefa, Sofia and I were sitting together in the kitchen. Sofia was making tortillas and Josefa was helping her shape them by clapping the dough between her hands.

'I knew a woman who went to jail just because her son-in-law wanted to steal her house away. It worked,' Sofia said. 'He is living in that house and the poor woman is in jail. The daughter visits her mother every Sunday, but cannot get her out. And she won't leave her husband because then they will really lose the house.'

'Salt,' Josefa answered as she chewed on a piece of the raw dough, making loud smacking sounds.

'I also know of another woman, who is called Visitation,' Sofia continued. 'She used to work at a bakery near here and I used to talk to her every time I went to buy bread. Her daughter-in-law was made of bile instead of blood.'

'Urine,' Josefa added.

'She told Visitation that her son was dying, but that he didn't want to worry his mother and, therefore, hadn't told her,' Sofia said. 'He'd worked for a large company from the United States making batteries for car motors. Her daughter-in-law said that this had made him sick. The daughter-in-law gave the son all kinds of teas to cure him and Visitation helped her do it. Of course, these teas were really poisons. When the son died, the daughter-in-law called the police and showed them how the mother had killed him. She'd kept all the teas in a large supermarket bag.'

'Tongue,' Josefa said.

'Yes,' Sofia answered. 'Visitation's son had a black tongue when he died.'

'What happened to the daughter-in-law?' I asked.

'Oh, she is fine,' Sofia answered. 'She is living in the

same house with one of the policemen who arrested Visitation.'

'Next,' Josefa added.

'Yes,' Sofia said, 'That policeman will be next.'

Two days after Leonora was taken to jail my mother took off her pyjamas, got dressed, and said she wanted to take me shopping. This was the first time that I could remember seeing her dressed and I thought that she looked very beautiful, but she seemed like a stranger. She bought me a yellow dress with a pattern of tiny, white triangles all over it. She bought herself the same dress, but in a larger size.

'Now we can look like twins,' she said. She also promised me that from now on she was going to be a good mother and take me out for lunch and to the movies. 'We will also go to church on Sundays,' she added.

When we got home from the shop, my father was standing in the kitchen talking to Sofia and Josefa. I could see he was very angry. His hands were knotted into fists and his front teeth were clenched tightly together. My mother took one look at him and ran out of the room. My father left the kitchen and followed her up to the bedroom taking two steps at a time.

'Now what is going to happen?' Sofia said, sitting down at the kitchen table and folding her hands in front of her.

We heard the bedroom door slam shut and then an awful silence as if the air had been blown out of the house.

'Misfortune,' Josefa said.

'I hope he beats her,' Sofia added.

SOME THINGS WERE OVERHEARD AND SOME SAID IT WAS ALL A RUMOUR

Then let mine arm fall from my shoulder blade,
and mine arm be broken from the bone.

At the jail five things happened to Leonora: her photograph was taken with her name scrawled on a blackboard and hung around her neck; her thumb print was registered in a large book; she was given a medical examination; she was told to put on some orange overalls; and she was taken to a small room that had two bunk-beds and a hole in the floor to be used as a toilet.

There were eight women in each cell so two women had to share one narrow bed. Everything was made of cement, even the beds. The room smelled like chlorine, mold, and watermelon rinds.

The first night Leonora lay in bed and picked at her smallpox scar until it bled. In the dark, the women in her cell asked her why she was in jail and Leonora told them what had happened.

'I did not do it,' Leonora protested. 'I have never stolen anything. I am not made like that.'

I am made of sinew and bone.
Swords and knives do not fit inside my hands.
I cannot hold an axe.

One of the women laughed and said, 'None of us should be here. None of us did it. We're are all trying to find the way out, and it isn't by going through the front gate!'

For there is hope of a tree, if it be cut down, that it will sprout again, and that the tender branch thereof will not cease.

In the morning Leonora woke up very early before the sun rose. In the distance she could hear the early-morning sound of the street sweeper as he brushed up leaves and dust in drawn-out, strong strokes along the sidewalks.

Leonora spent three days and two nights in jail before Mr. O'Conner posted bail. A policewoman came to the cell and asked Leonora to follow her to a small room where she gave Leonora her clothes and told her to change out of her prison uniform. Then she led her to an office where she was told to sign some documents. After doing this, Leonora was told she could leave. Mr. O'Conner was waiting in the rain for her, outside the prison gate. He was standing under a large, black umbrella. He walked toward Leonora, held the umbrella over her head, and guided her to the car.

'This is the beginning of the rainy season,' he said.

Leonora did not answer.

In the car on the way back to the house, Mr. O'Conner said, 'You just have to forget this ever happened.'

'I did not steal the ring. I promise,' Leonora answered. She could not even cry. She felt dry and cold like a stone as she listened to the sound of the car's windshield wipers slipping back and forth against the glass. It sounded like a song to her. It sounded like, 'Fall. Stop. Fall. Stop. Fall. Stop.'

Leonora could smell the musty, humid scent of the jail on her arms as though it had permeated her skin. Her thumb was still coated in black ink. She could feel the prison doctor's hands on her skin touching her neck and wrists. She could taste cement on her lips.

'Of course you didn't. But never steal anything again,' Mr. O'Conner answered in a stern voice.

He giveth snow like wool.
Who can stand before his cold?

Leonora could hear Mrs. O'Conner's thoughts move across the city's streets, over and around buildings and into Leonora's mind. Mrs. O'Conner was thinking, 'Ah. I am carried by the river.'

Mr. O'Conner sighed and said, 'You know, Leonora, this breaks my heart, but I think it might be best for you to leave. It will be the best for all of us, even for you. It might make Mrs. O'Conner get well again . . .'

'No!' Leonora interrupted. She thought this was the very first time in her life that she had ever said that word – an obstinate, mule word. A word for small mouths.

'We want you out in a week,' he said.

I could stand like a cross.

'But what about Aura?' Leonora asked. 'What about my daughter? What about Aura Olivia?'

'You are still very young,' Mr. O'Conner answered. 'And you are very pretty. Did I ever tell you that? I am sure that I did tell you that. You will have many suitors, you will get married and then you can have more children.'

Leonora shook her head. 'No one in my family has ever married,' she said in a whisper.

'You can forget Aura,' Mr. O'Conner continued in a gentle voice. 'You know I love her and she will have the best of everything. You will forget her in the same way you forget a dream. It will take some time . . .'

I am carried by the river.

When they arrived at the house Leonora quickly got out of the car and ran straight up to the servants' room on the roof. Sofia was sitting on Leonora's bed waiting for her. Sofia opened her arms, embraced Leonora, and rocked her like a child.

'Mrs. O'Conner went too far,' Sofia said, 'She must have placed that ring under your pillow when she came upstairs to sit with us and watch television. I called Mr. O'Conner's secretary immediately and told her what had happened. She located him and so he returned.'

'Thank you,' Leonora said quietly.

'Yes, you can thank me for getting you out of there so soon,' Sofia answered.

A green stick shreds,
it cannot break.

'Sofia, listen to me,' Leonora sighed. She took a deep breath and moved away from Sofia. 'I have to leave here. Mr. O'Conner says that I have to leave. I feel filled with shame. I have to leave with Aura. I am going to run away with her.'

'Stop that nonsense right now!' Sofia said. 'You cannot do that. Then you will go to jail for ever. They'll say you kidnapped her. You don't have any money. Where are you going to go?'

'I have to think very carefully,' Leonora said.

'And, after all, what makes you think Aura wants to go with you?' Sofia continued. 'Aura will never want to leave. This is madness. Pure madness!'

'Aura loves me,' Leonora protested. 'And deep inside she knows that I am the one who loves her, who protects her. She knows . . .'

> *I am the memory of the future. My daughter knows*
> *the scent that is her own. Arms that are baskets.*
> *She knows the shade*
> *under my wing.*

EVERY LEAF IS A MOUTH

A few days ago Leonora came back from jail. My mother did not come downstairs to see her. Instead, we could hear my mother walk backward and forward in her room. From downstairs we listened to loud sounds as if she were moving the furniture around or cleaning out her drawers. Sometimes it sounded as if things were being broken. When I'd go and knock on her door she'd say, 'Come back later.'

She wouldn't let my father into the room either. Every time he knocked on the door she said she was getting a surprise ready for him.

'Come back later,' she'd cry out. 'Not yet. THE CATS.'

I thought she was beginning to act a little bit like Josefa. When I mentioned this to Sofia she said, 'No, Aura, you don't understand. She's not acting like Josefa, she's acting more like Leonora.'

'No,' I answered. 'How can you say that? She's nothing like Leonora.'

'Maybe you don't think so,' Sofia said. 'But I see two women who are in each others' skin.'

'What do you mean?' I asked.

'Never mind. Some things are visible and some are invisible,' Sofia answered and walked out of the room.

Sometimes she really irritates me.

This morning I finally saw Leonora. I was in the garden under the grapefruit tree when she came outside walking very slowly, with one foot directly in front of the other, like an Indian. She sat beside me.

'Was the jail bad?' I asked.

'Not so bad,' Leonora answered.

Leonora circled one arm around me. 'It is good to see you,' she said. 'You look very pretty.' I was wearing the new yellow dress with the triangle print my mother had bought me.

Leonora told me that she did not steal my mother's ring. She said that she would never steal anything because she knew all the Psalms.

'Do you believe me?' she asked.

'Yes,' I said. 'Of course I believe you.'

After we had sat together for a few minutes, Leonora leaned over and placed her ear against my mouth. She smelled like lemon and watermelon. She clutched a handful of grass in her fist, as if she were holding on to the Earth.

'Why don't we just run away together,' she whispered. She said it very slowly so it sounded like: 'Why. Don't. We. Run. Away. Together?'

I laughed. It sounded funny. Then I turned my head and whispered back into her ear, 'No. I. Cannot. Leave,' I said, imitating her.

'Why not?' Leonora asked, leaning away from me and holding my chin with her hand.

'Leonora,' I explained. 'I can't leave my family.'

'I am your family,' she answered.

'You are a part of the family,' I explained. 'But my mother and father are my *real* family.'

Leonora said she had thought about it for a while and that she had saved all the money she had earned.

'Since you were born,' Leonora told me, 'I have never spent my earnings. I have not even bought myself one single hair ribbon. You've seen that my braids are held together with rubber-bands.'

She said that we could take a taxi, a bus, or even a train. She said that she was sure I would love to ride in a train.

I reminded her that I had already been on a train when I had gone on a vacation to Guadalajara.

Leonora shook her head. She said that my name sounded like a deep well and that someone might try to climb inside me.

'I cannot leave. Please listen. My house is here, my bed is here,' I said. 'And, after all, you are a servant!' I added.

Leonora closed her eyes and began to tremble. She continued to clutch the handful of grass. She rocked back and forth and leaned away from me.

'Please, open your eyes!' I said. 'What is the matter? Look at me!'

I felt frightened. She looked sick.

Leonora opened her eyes. I could see the shadows of the

grapefruit tree above us reflected in her black eyes. She touched my mouth with her fingers and said, 'Aura, you are under my arm. How can anything be bad when you are here under my arm?'

SOME THINGS WERE OVERHEARD AND
SOME SAID IT WAS ALL A RUMOUR

I am a broom-child. My voice sounds like sweeping. Comb, rake, brush, sweep against stone, dirt, and grass. Dry, brittle sound. Scratch. A rasp and scrape without vowels. A long shhhhhhhhh.

A wreath of fingers. Tearing a green stick. We know how to be quiet. Our thoughts are whispers.

They say there is no honey in this land.

Only the cross does not steal because it cannot move its arms.

The stones bled when the virgin died.

Listen for whistles, listen for tambourines. I will walk where I have never walked before and breathe unfamiliar air. I will stand at a window. I will open a door. I will open my hand, open my mouth, and swallow a new house.

Break a stick. Taste the marrow. Pray to the Virgin. Light a candle.

Bark stripped off of wood.
She is so clean.
She is so soft.
She is like bread.
Clean, soft bread.

The land will not be fallow. The rain will come.
Bouquets of fingers.
Brick walls, stone walls, cement walls, adobe walls.
There is no honey in this land.
The house tastes like tangerines, yellow plastic buckets,
and linseed oil. It smells of soap and coriander.
Bite a twig if you want to come home.
Talking about the day time.
Starched, white aprons hang over chairs.
A shadow does not move.
The house bends over me and carries my feet when I
walk. The stairs lift me and hold me high.

Innocent little dove, you have let yourself be fooled,
knowing that on this day you should lend nothing.
Until tomorrow.

I want to go to your country so you may sing your songs to
me.

Everyone finds a tree.

The dry taste of a stone covered in dust. The cool taste of a blue pebble. Rock like ice. Rock like salt. The taste of sun and clay. A riverbed inside.

Boat of silver, how silently you glide away from the old shore. White sea gulls, white handkerchiefs.

Tell the little cow she has a calf at her feet and she is breeding another. Tell the little cow to come down to the road. She has a calf at her feet and she is breeding another.
Whisper. Wind. Sweep. Angel bless this house. Let me in.

   Taste the marrow.
   Brooms on stone. Brooms on grass and brick.

Timorous body why get frightened? Cowardly body, don't be afraid. May she not die in childbirth, may she not die of fright, may she not die without confession; may that fright fall in the ocean, may it fall into the mountains, may it seize another unfortunate.

The virgin deer. The virgin cow. The virgin dog.
Breathe on glass. Breathe into the cup of your hand. Pray for cobblers and iron-welders. Pray for all the virgin animals.

Spit and water.

   I feel my whole body in my mouth. My legs, arms and

hands are in my mouth. My liver and spleen are in
my mouth. My breasts are in my mouth.
Empty clothes. Scarecrow. Arms and legs made of
branches. A broomstick is a spine. A leaf is a mouth.
Don't be afraid. You are the sailor's guide. Today I
come to greet you, greeting your beauty in your
celestial reign.
The broom-children are out there asleep under a tree.
They are surrounded by bundles of twigs tied with
yarn. This night also belongs to them.

In this city there is no darkness, or night. No
where to see the moon and stars. There
are no night sounds. There is no place to
hide.
Hide beneath an arm.
I can cup my hands over my eyes.
The night is in my hands.
Sweet Virgin, please.
What can I bring to this place?
Crystal dove, glass dove, dove made from a
window pane. I do not want to break you. I
do not want to break you. Crystal dove I
do not want you in pieces, broken on the
floor.
If the dog barks: listen.
If the cat cries: listen.
If the birds sing: listen.
The doors creak.

The windows murmur.
The floors whisper.
Everything speaks.

Like a tree planted by the rivers of water.

I hear a sweet voice. I hear a voice in the trees. It is
    not the breeze. It is not the sound of wings.
The statues of the Lord are right, rejoicing the heart.

Let the words of my mouth.
There is no speech nor language where their voice is
    not heard.
Blessed be my rock.
To bleed the blackness out and clean its dark, dark
    smell of bark and monkey.
I may tell all my bones: they look and stare upon me.

Quiet, peace. Close your eyes
and don't open them
until I tell you.

Be not far from me; for trouble is near; for there is
    none to help.

28 days.
28 stairs to the roof.
His breathing sounds like his own breath.
Drink new water.

I will let the rain fall. Let the river take the leaf. Let the wind move the leaf. Sweep the leaf.

Aloe. Alum. Ammonia. Bitter apple. Borax. Camphor. Cotton root bark. Laburnum. Lead. Oil of thyme. Oleander leaves and bark. Quinine. Salts of arsenic. Slippery elm sticks. Yew.

Before only God knew.
Before only God knew and protected me.
Sleep with stones. Stones can bleed.

I am two. There are two hearts, two livers and four kidneys inside of me. I have four legs and four arms. I have four eyes and two mouths. I am two.

Run rabbit run. Fly bird fly.
A spool of thread unwinding. The sound before rain.
They part my garments among them.

He said my name. Slap. Thunder. Butterfly.
Blessing. Blessing bark. Lead me in a plain path.
Everybody knows.

Twigs tearing. A green stick tearing. Slap. Thunder. Butterfly. Crystal dove, glass dove, dove made from a window pane. I do not want to break you. I do not want to break you. Crystal dove I do not want you in pieces, broken on the floor.

The fly began to sing
Everyone was quiet,
It was a song
No one could hear.

Let the field be joyful, and all that is therein: then
*   shall all the trees of the wood rejoice.*
He stepped on my shadow. I could not walk. And
*   then I could not breath. I did not know what had*
*   happened until it happened. It was like trying to*
*   stop the rain. It was like holding a broom.*
No.
Let my cry come unto thee.
. . . withered like grass; so that I forget to eat
*   my bread.*

Blood is thicker than milk, it turns hard in a few
*   minutes. Blood becomes a stone.*
Like an animal, like a cow in a barn. I am two. Two
*   hearts, two mouths, two livers.*
I am a pelican of the wilderness.
I watch, and am as a sparrow alone upon the
*   house top.*
Where I come from, there is only one room. There is
*   one room, one life.*
I have eaten ashes like bread.
Sing unto him a new song; play skilfully with a
*   loud noise.*
My moisture is turned into the drought of summer.

Mary, receive the flowers; Mary, receive the flowers
that are so pure and beautiful and with them my
prayers, and with them my prayers.

Show me thy ways, O lord; teach me thy paths.
The troubles of my heart are enlarged.

In the secret of his tabernacle shall he hide me;
He shall set me up upon a rock.

The baby is mine too. Broom-child. Tree child.

I am a mother. A seed shall serve him.
I will wash my hands in innocency.

He hath put a new song in my mouth.
It moves in me. Does it weep in me? It feels like a
broom, softly sweeping bread crumbs.

The dark Virgin.
Nothing hurts. The whole world is in me. O ye gates;
even lift them up, ye everlasting doors.

Pluck my feet out of the net.
Try my reins and my heart.
My foot standeth in an even place.

Hearken O daughter; and consider,
And incline thine ear; forget also thine own people,
And thy father's house.

Stand with your head bowed to the sky. Kneel. Kiss
the ground.

Broom-child. Good morning dark dove, today I
come to greet you, greeting your beauty in your
celestial reign.

I want to remember all the songs I know.
Women at the river, beating stones, washing against
stones. Hearts beat against stones. The fabric bleeds
in the water. Blue, blue, orange, red in the river.
The heart bleeds in the river. Rag and blouse, rag
and stone beat in the river.
Arms in the river. Braids in the river.

Give ear to my prayer.
My heart is a leaf on the ground.

Hummingbird.

Harvest.

Can you keep a secret? No one is looking?

Like an animal, like a cow in a barn.
Thou tellest my wonderings; put thou
My tears into thy bottle: are they not in
Thy book?

Timorous body why get frightened? Cowardly body,
don't be afraid. I stretch out my arms. There is a
cross in me. Drink. Swallow the river and clouds. I
can taste the day I was born.

I am a mirror. A secret. The best mother.

The rings on a tree. Circles around the tree trunk.
Hoops, bands. Wedding rings.

How can anyone walk in the garden? The garden of
dead cats. He held my arm and told me I could
do it. He said I could do it because I had an
Indian heart and my hands were strong. I am not
so strong,
but stronger than I thought.

Meet me at the river.

Obey. Touch my shoulder. No one will look at my
back. No one will see the back of my arms and neck
walking away. No one will hear me close the door
and my steps walking down the street.

I sing that I may be heard, not because my voice is
good. Let their eyes not see me, let their feet not
reach me, may their hands not touch me. I sing that
I may be heard.
No answer.

Let me in. Let me in. Let me in.

A broom stick
can be a body
to embrace.

They that sit in the gate speak against
me; and I was the song of the drunkards.
The plowers plowed upon my back;
They made long their furrows.

Lift up your hands in the sanctuary.

That our daughters may be
as corner stones,
polished after the similitude of a palace.

Rid me, and deliver me from the hand
Of strange children,
Whose mouth speaketh vanity,
And their right hand
Is a right hand of falsehood.

A wishing well. Charm. Talisman. Amulet.

Remember the song.
One child fell in the wishing well
and then they covered it up.
The child drowned in the wishing well

and then they covered it up.
They covered it up with stones and board,
with stones and boards,
with stones and boards,
but the child still cries
and weeps for home.

The grapefruits fall from the tree like stones.

Do not make anyone angry.

And thy mercy cut off mine enemies, and destroy all of
them that afflict my soul: for I am thy servant.

Before he takes his bow, his spear, his arrows,
He will not touch me,
Fearing to make them jealous:
The jaguar, the monkey, the deer.
I too am like the animals,
When he hunts I cry.

Then let mine arm fall from my shoulder blade,
And mine arm be broken from the bone.

I am made of sinew and bone.
Swords and knives do not fit inside my hands.
I cannot hold an axe.

For there is hope of a tree, if it be cut down, that

it will sprout again, and that the tender branch
thereof will not cease.

He giveth snow like wool.
Who can stand before his cold?

I could stand like a cross.

I am carried by the river.
A green stick shreds,
it cannot break.

I am the memory of her future. My daughter knows
The scent that is her own. Arms that are baskets.
She knows the shade
Under my wing.

EVERY LEAF IS A MOUTH

Now my right hand wants to dig. It scratches at everything.

Two days later my father, Josefa, Sofia, and I were sitting in the kitchen. My father kept asking Sofia to explain everything again, even though she'd already told us four times.

Sofia said that the first thing she noticed missing was the long, blue clothesline. The clothes that had been hung out to dry were lying all over the roof. Since there had been no wind for days, Sofia thought this was strange.

'Then, I went downstairs,' Sofia said. 'To find what I was looking for.'

Sofia discovered Leonora's body lying in the garden under the grapefruit tree.

She explained that she could see everything as it had happened, as though the air in the garden still held the picture for her. Sofia could see my mother going outside very early in the morning and pulling Leonora down from the grapefruit tree. Then, Sofia explained, my mother knelt down and, after drawing the clothesline off Leonora's neck, she tied it around her own.

Sofia said that now we all needed to walk more slowly.

Josefa said, 'Who will get their clothes?'

Everyone was quiet.

It was five words.